THE
TWIN FLAME
REALITY

Also by Michelle Gordon:

Fiction
The Girl Who Loved Too Much

Earth Angel Series
The Earth Angel Training Academy
The Earth Angel Awakening
The Other Side
The Twin Flame Reunion
The Twin Flame Retreat
The Twin Flame Resurrection
The Twin Flame Reality
The Twin Flame Rebellion
The Twin Flame Reignition
The Twin Flame Resolution
The Old Soul's Handbook

Visionary Collection
Heaven dot com
The Doorway to PAM
The Elphite
I'm Here

Children's Fiction
The Magical Faerie Door

Poetry
Duelling Poets

Non-fiction
Where's My F**king Unicorn?

THE TWIN FLAME REALITY

MICHELLE GORDON

Faerie published in Great Britain in 2016 by The Amethyst Angel
Angel Edition published in 2017 by The Amethyst Angel

ISBN: 978-1-912257-07-2

Publication mentioned – Freedom Inside – freedominside.com

Angel Edition

This book is dedicated to you.
You are a brave, beautiful, wise Earth Angel, and you
deserve all the love, happiness and joy you desire.
If things seem a little dark right now, then please know
that this too, shall pass.
I love you.

CHAPTER ONE

Lisa felt the energy flow through her fingertips and into the body of her client, who was resting comfortably on the massage couch. She breathed deeply and opened herself up fully to the flow of divine light that was shining down on them both. A deep feeling of peace settled upon her, and her body shook at the intensity of the energy that she was channelling. She could see the light was healing and energising every cell of the body of the man lying in front of her, and she felt exhilarated at the thought that he may have less pain by the time the session finished.

What felt like hours later, but really was only about thirty minutes, Lisa felt the light dimming, and the energy receding. She thanked the Angels for their assistance, and drew back from her connection to the universal energy. She took in several deep breaths, then stepped back and reached to touch the floor, to ground any excess energy.

She sat down in her chair to meditate while her client came round.

"Wow," he said, sitting up slowly, blinking and

stretching. "What happened?"

Lisa smiled. "It was quite a strong energy coming through, you may feel something of a healing crisis in your body for the next day or two, but I think you will feel much better after that."

"I hate to sound cynical, but we'll have to see. I've had this back pain for two years now, and nothing has worked."

"I have helped to give your body the energy it needs to heal, but perhaps we need to do something else too, before you leave." She glanced at the clock, she still had five minutes before she had to prepare for her next client.

"The back pain has become a story, part of who you are. In order to heal the back pain, it would be a good idea to let go of the story, don't you think?"

Her client frowned. "I'm not sure I follow you."

"It doesn't matter, just copy my actions and repeat after me."

Her client nodded and she began to tap on the side of her hand. "Even though I have back pain, I totally love and accept myself."

He copied her words and actions, and after a few minutes, she could see his posture change, and his facial features begin to relax. She knew that the combination of the energy healing and the tapping would help his body to realign itself, and the pain would go away.

She said goodbye to him, noting that he was definitely more upright now than he was when he'd arrived.

"You can really see the difference," Ruby commented.

Lisa nodded to the owner of the crystal shop where she rented the therapy room once a week.

"He'll be fine. I've asked him to let me know how he

feels, but I'll probably never hear from him again. Once people lose the pain, they forget it even existed and move onto other things."

"It's amazing that they get better so quickly, but it would be nice to get the feedback. Do you want a cuppa before the next client? She's due in a few minutes."

"Yes, please," Lisa said to Ruby. "I'll just get everything ready."

"Okay," Ruby said, going into the kitchen to get the kettle on.

Lisa went back to the therapy room and cleared it using her singing bowl and some incense. She asked the Angels to sweep through energetically, and remove anything that her previous client had left behind.

"She's here," Ruby said, poking her head around the door and holding a mug out to Lisa. Lisa took the tea and nodded.

"You can send her in, I'm ready."

There was a delicate knock at the door moments later, and Lisa opened the door, but her greeting died in her throat. She gestured to the chair, and her client crossed the room and sat down. "Thank you so much for fitting me in, I understand you don't often have spaces available, which is a good sign for a healer I guess!"

Lisa nodded, wondering why she was having such a strange reaction to the woman's presence. She sat down and sipped her tea, then managed to speak. "Have we met before?"

The woman smiled. "I don't think so. Though I do get asked that often."

Lisa looked down at the form the woman had filled in

when she booked the session. "Your name is Violet, and you're an author?"

Violet nodded. "Yes, though I've only written one book so far."

Lisa frowned. "Is it the one that Ruby stocks here?"

Violet smiled. "Yes, that's the one. I've known Ruby for a while. She helps to advertise the Twin Flame Retreat that I run, just up the road from here."

"I've not read the book yet, I keep meaning to though."

"You will read it when you're meant to," Violet said with a smile. "It won't make sense if you try to read it before you're ready."

"I agree with you there," Lisa said. "Everything must happen at the right moment. Now then, what can I help you with today?" she asked, scanning the form and not seeing any red flags or reasons why Violet might have sought her aid.

Violet sighed. "There's nothing wrong, or at least, I don't think there is. It's just that I've been married for six years now, and in all that time, we've never conceived. Of course, we've only been a little more lax about contraception in recent years, but as it's never happened I wondered if there was something stopping it."

"What does your doctor say about it?" Lisa asked, making some notes on Violet's form.

"I don't trust doctors, so I'm afraid I haven't been to see one about it. I would rather explore alternative routes."

Lisa nodded. "That's understandable, though it might still be a good idea for both of you to get checked out and see if there are any issues."

"Okay, well, if it comes to that, I will."

"Good." Lisa put the papers down and stood, motioning to the massage couch. "Why don't you lie down on your back and get comfortable, and we'll see what comes up. I tend to work with the Angels to channel energy and to receive any images or words they wish for me to see."

Violet nodded and got up onto the couch, slipping off her shoes as she did so. She lay back and got comfortable, then closed her eyes.

"Just relax, I'm going to play some music quietly so that your mind has something to focus on, and your thoughts calm down."

Violet smiled, but didn't open her eyes. Lisa pressed play on her iPod, then stood beside the couch, bare feet digging into the soft rug, her knees slightly bent and relaxed and her hands hovering above Violet's abdomen.

She closed her eyes, and almost immediately she was given images. They were flying through her mind so fast, it was difficult to focus on any one in particular.

She asked the Angels to slow them down, and allow her to see them properly, and one of the images came into focus, then began to move like it was a film.

She saw Violet clothed in purple robes, stood on a stage. She seemed to be teaching a class of people that Lisa herself was sat amongst. Though intrigued by the scene, Lisa asked the Angels to take her to the root of Violet's problem with conceiving. No sooner than she made the request, she found herself zooming toward Violet, and entering her heart.

The images came fast again, and Lisa asked the Angels to slow it down. She found herself standing in front of a large glass window, facing the beach, at night. She looked out to the inky sky and the stars shone brightly like jewels.

Lisa couldn't remember ever seeing them so bright before.

She focused on the two people in front of her, and asked the Angels to allow her to hear their conversation.

"So there is a way to avoid this fate?"

"For most, yes."

Their voices were faint, and Lisa found herself moving closer to hear them better. When the woman turned to face the man, her features came into focus, and Lisa recognised the woman as being Violet.

"What do you mean, for most?" the man asked.

Lisa could see the pain in Violet's eyes as she replied. "For you. You will be saved."

"But not you?"

Violet shook her head, and Lisa saw her place her hand on her stomach. "Nor our child."

The scene changed, and suddenly Lisa was on the beach. It was daylight, but the skies were an ugly colour, the ground did not feel stable under her feet.

She looked along the shore and saw Violet and the man again, though she was shocked to see that Violet had aged horribly, that her hair was white, her body was ravaged, and her skin wrinkled.

She moved closer to the couple, unseen by them.

"Don't make me leave, my love," the man begged her. "Please don't send me away to the seas. Let me stay here, be with you until the end."

Violet shook her head. "No, they need you, you must go. They will need a strong leader, a Seer, a healer. Without you, they will not thrive."

Her voice was weak, and her body was trembling.

"But how will I thrive without you?" the man asked,

tears running down his cheeks. "I love you, I'll love you for eternity."

Violet smiled. "Our love will outlast eternity itself." She reached up to wipe away his tears, then she reached out her arms and he gathered her thin frame into an embrace.

Lisa felt tears prickle her own eyes as she watched them. The love between them was almost visible. She saw Violet touch his neck, then a shudder went through her body, and her spirit left her. The man let out a wail and gripped her body tightly to him as he sank to his knees.

"I love you, please don't leave me," he sobbed, as he smoothed her white hair.

He appeared to be gasping, short of breath. Lisa noticed that his legs were turning into a tail, and there were gills on his neck.

He kissed Violet's lifeless lips, then set her body on the sand and bowed his head. "Goodbye, my love."

The ground began to shake and he moved away from Violet toward the sea. When he was a few metres out, he looked back to the beach one more time, then he disappeared into the waves.

Lisa heard the Angels call her back then, and she breathed deeply and re-entered her body in the therapy room. Her hands were shaking, and she opened her eyes and looked down at Violet's closed eyes and peaceful expression. She noticed that a tear had fallen and slid down Violet's face. Had she sensed what Lisa had just witnessed?

Lisa grounded the excess energy and thanked the Angels for their assistance, then she sat down in her chair and sipped her cold tea. She glanced at her clock and was shocked to see that the session was nearly over. Had she been inside Violet's memories for nearly an hour? Time had taken on an odd quality.

She looked up to see Violet stirring.

"Sit up slowly," she cautioned her client. "Take your time. I have a break between you and the next appointment, there's no rush."

Violet blinked then shifted about on the couch and slowly sat up, groaning a little at the stiffness in her limbs from being so still.

"What happened?" she asked. "I was getting flashes of images, but I couldn't get a hold of any of them. Were you able to see anything?"

Lisa nodded. She motioned to the chair opposite her, and poured Violet a glass of water. Violet sat down and sipped the water.

"I was getting quick flashes too, so I asked the Angels to slow them down, in order for me to understand."

"Good idea," Violet said, nodding. "Didn't think of that."

"I saw you, on a stage, in purple robes, teaching a large group of people."

Violet nodded, not looking in the slightest bit surprised.

"Then I asked to be shown the root of your problem, and I was taken to a house by the beach, where I saw you standing in the window, with a man who had long blond hair. You told him that he would be saved, but you would not." Lisa sighed. "And neither would your child. You were pregnant."

Violet's eyes widened as she took this information in.

"Then I was taken to another memory, where you were on the beach with the same man, and you had aged, your hair was white, your body thin and ravaged. He was begging you to let him stay, to be with you, but instead you turned him into a Merman and then died in his arms."

Tears were streaming down Violet's face, and Lisa pulled out a tissue from the box beside her and handed it over.

Violet took it and wiped her eyes, looking a little shocked. "So the reason we are not conceiving now is because when we were together before, I lost the baby, and then died?"

Lisa nodded. "You recognise the blond man as the man you are with now?"

"Yes, he is my Twin Flame." Violet was silent for a while. "It makes sense. I have had memories of him telling me about that moment in our last encounter on the Other Side. But he never mentioned I was pregnant when it happened. And I had blocked most of my memories from that time. From our life together in Atlantis."

Lisa's eyebrows raised. "That was Atlantis? Those memories I saw, on the beach?"

"Yes, when the people were turned into Merpeople and escaped the end of the world."

"Goddess," Lisa said. "That's incredible."

"So is there any way of healing that pain? Of removing the block to us conceiving in this life? Or are we just never meant to have a child?"

"I didn't ask the Angels that," Lisa admitted. "I have always believed that almost anything can be healed and resolved, but it depends on how willing we are to let it go." She heard a whisper then, and she frowned. "I'm getting the message that it's not so much that you have to let it go, it's that your Flame does. The pain of losing his unborn child, and then you, has marked him deeply, and he is unwilling to risk losing you both again."

Violet nodded. "That makes sense." She sighed. "How can I bring that up with him though, and get him to release it?"

"You could suggest that he come to see me," Lisa said. "I can't promise anything, but I can see if there's anything I can do to help."

Violet smiled. "Thank you, I may well do just that." She slipped her shoes on and stood up. "I don't want to take up any more of your time, I know it's meant to be your break right now. Do I pay at the counter?"

Lisa nodded. "Yes, that's great. And you are most welcome, I have enjoyed our session, please feel free to come back if you wish to."

"I will." Violet moved toward the door.

"Wait," Lisa said. "In the memory of you on the stage, in the purple robes, it felt like I was really there myself, not just witnessing your memory. Is that how I know you? Is that where we met before?"

Violet grinned. "Grab a copy of my book, and see for yourself," she said.

Lisa nodded. "I will. Thanks." She watched Violet leave the room, then sat back in the chair and finished her cold tea.

When she had arrived at the shop that morning, she'd had no idea that the day would be quite so interesting.

CHAPTER TWO

"It's barely November, is it really necessary to have Christmas stuff in the shops already?"

Quentin turned to see his girlfriend looking at him with her eyebrows raised. "What is your problem with Christmas?" she asked. "You complained about it last year, and the year before. Now it's only November second and you're already complaining about it."

Though he could hear the teasing tone in her voice, her words riled him up a little. He wasn't complaining about Christmas, he was complaining about having to see the decorations and hear the music nearly two months before the actual occasion. What was wrong with that?

"Whatever," he muttered, turning away to move to another aisle. He saw the smile slip off Jenna's face and he regretted his brush-off. Unable to admit that he was wrong, he continued on his rant. "It's just such a waste of money, I mean, the whole thing is completely commercialised. When I was younger we were lucky to have a few small gifts in our stockings, the biggest gifts we had were spending time with our family and having time to relax."

"And because you had so little when you were younger, how dare children these days have more than you had? Why shouldn't they live in scarcity too?"

There was sarcasm in Jenna's tone this time, and it stirred up yet more feelings inside him. This time of anger. "That's not what I'm saying! I just don't see why it has to be all about plastic toys and cheap decorations! Where is the family aspect? Where is the joy in the more simple pleasures of the holiday?"

By now, they were stood in the middle of the busy department store aisle, and Quentin became aware that they were drawing the attention of the shoppers around them as their voices raised higher.

"I'm sure there are plenty of people who do spend time with their families, enjoying the simple pleasures! Just because *you* no longer do that, doesn't mean no one else does!"

His anger boiled over, but before he could reply, Jenna dumped her shopping basket on the floor and stormed away, the crowd parting for her as she left. Quentin took several deep breaths, and tried to control his irritation and frustration. He wanted to break something, but he didn't want to give anyone the satisfaction of watching him have a meltdown.

Once he felt more in control, he exited the store and then paused to figure out where Jenna would have gone. The smell of coffee hit his nostrils and he nodded. She had a particular fondness for the lattes in the coffee shop around the corner, so that seemed like the best place to start.

Within seconds of entering, he spotted her in the

corner, her back to him. He knew that he would need a peace offering of some kind, as the rational part of him kicked in and he realised that despite his annoyance with the music and decorations, starting an argument in public with Jenna had been a stupid thing to do.

He went to the counter and saw that they were selling Christmas cookies already. Though part of him was groaning, he found himself ordering two, and an Americano for himself.

He waited impatiently for his order to be made, then he went over to Jenna and set his offering on the table.

She looked down at the plate and her lips curved upwards.

"I come in peace," he said quietly, taking the seat opposite. He reached across to take her hand. "I'm so sorry, it was a ridiculous thing to get into an argument over, and I know that you hate public displays like that."

Jenna pulled the head off the snowman cookie and nodded. She chewed the cookie slowly and waited for him to continue.

"You're right, I don't do the family thing anymore, and it does bother me, because now it feels like Christmas is a time of painful memories and unfulfilled wishes. I really just wish I could go back to when I was a boy, when it was a time of anticipation and magic." Much to his horror, tears welled up in his eyes and a couple spilled down his cheeks. He hated public displays of emotion too. Today was just a washout on all accounts.

Jenna squeezed his hand back, unshed tears glistening in her eyes. "I'm sorry," she said. "I know that Christmas really pushes your buttons, but it hurts that you don't want to celebrate it, or enjoy it, because as a child I didn't have such a great time, I had to learn how to enjoy it as an adult. So I would really like to experience a good Christmas with you."

Quentin shook his head and dabbed his eyes with a napkin. "What are we like, eh?"

Jenna smiled and nibbled more of the snowman.

Quentin took a deep breath. "I propose that we make this Christmas the best one we've ever had. Let's go the whole hog."

Jenna raised an eyebrow. "I don't think we could eat a whole hog between us."

Quentin chuckled and the tension evaporated. He loved her quirky sense of humour. He wished he had just seen the humour in the situation earlier and not got into such a public mess.

"Have we got a deal?" he asked, holding his hand out.

Jenna nodded and shook his hand. "We will make this Christmas the best ever."

"Excellent. Now, let's drink up, eat our cookies and then go and find the best fairy lights we can. I'm pretty sure that they didn't work last year, and I didn't bother to replace them."

"Sounds like a plan," Jenna said, sipping her coffee. "Can we get a real tree this time too?"

All of the hassle that came with a real tree came to Quentin's mind, and he had to count to three before responding, because his immediate reaction would have been a resounding 'no'. The pain of the needles everywhere, the daily watering so it didn't die, and then trying to make it stand upright in a pot? All of those things filled him with dread, but he was aware that Jenna loved to have a real tree. She loved the smell of the pine needles.

Before he could think it through too hard, he nodded and quickly bit the head off the Santa cookie so he didn't have to articulate a positive response.

Jenna beamed at him, and his heart melted. "Awesome!"

*   *   *

"Do you ever get tired?"

Pearl smiled at the Angel stood by her side at the gates and shook her head. "Not really. I know that it may seem like a perpetually long day here, since we don't need sleep and there are no breaks, but it doesn't feel tiring or boring to me."

The Angel, a newly returned soul called Zoisite, frowned. "But most of the time, you're just standing here. You don't find that boring?"

Pearl chuckled. "I can tell you have not long returned from Earth, dear Angel. I know that humans see it as something of a crime to just be, to stand still and do nothing, but here in the Angelic Realm it is not. Though it may appear I am doing nothing, in truth, I am connecting to the Universe. I am in flow with the energies around me, I am being grounded and filling myself with light so that I may best serve each soul who arrives here from Earth, or indeed from anywhere else in the Universe."

"Wow, I guess when you put it that way, you're not standing around doing nothing after all."

"No, I'm not," Pearl agreed. "But I want to make it clear to you – standing around 'doing nothing' is not a crime, it is in fact a very good thing to do. To rest, completely rest, is good for the soul. And for humans, I don't mean sleeping rest. I mean just being, and not trying to accomplish anything in particular."

"They call that meditation," Zoisite said. "I tried to do it, but I wasn't very good at it."

"I can tell that it may be an issue for you," Pearl said wryly. "But actually, what humans call mediation is not quite what I mean, after all, there is usually an intention, an expected outcome to meditation, whether it's to relax or allow creative ideas to flow or to clear your mind. I'm talking about really doing nothing. Just a few minutes of doing zilch, with no need for those minutes to mean anything or result in anything."

"Huh," Zoisite said. "I can't remember doing anything like that on Earth."

"I know, there are very few people who do. I personally think that it would be very beneficial for them if they did."

"Does it bother you that I'm disturbing you right now?" Zoisite asked suddenly after a few moments of silence.

Pearl shook her head. "Of course not, Angel. You are not disturbing me in the slightest, I enjoy the company. Have you decided what you would like to do here in the Angelic Realm?"

Zoisite smiled. "After this conversation, I have decided that the very first thing I would like to do is absolutely nothing. Then, once I have tried that, I will see how I feel."

"Wise choice," Pearl said. "Be sure to pop by and let me know how it goes."

Zoisite reached out to hug her, then walked away from the gates, down the path that led to the lake.

Pearl watched the Angel go, a smile on her face. She wondered what it would be like to be so full of questions, so full of curiosity and desire to know things. Being completely connected to the divine as she was, feelings of bliss and peace were all she really knew. Everything else was just conceptual to her.

She wondered if she should have taken up the offer to go to Earth to be with her Flame. Many Earthly years before, she had been given the chance, but she felt it was more important for her to be here, fulfilling her role at the gates to the Angelic Realm.

But there were moments when she doubted her decision to stay. Had she stopped herself from being able to not just feel unconditional love, but to truly experience all that came with it?

"Penny for your thoughts."

Pearl turned around to see Gold standing in the mists. She reached out to embrace the Elder.

"We don't have pennies here," Pearl said with a smile as she released him.

"Of course we do," Gold said, reaching into his pocket and pulling out a small golden coin which he then gave to Pearl.

She smiled at the tiny disc, which had a '1' on one side and angel wings on the other.

"Thank you, well, seeing as you've paid, I was just thinking about whether I should have gone to Earth, to experience true love with my Twin Flame, rather than stay and fulfil my duty here."

Gold sighed and nodded. "I have often had the same thoughts, dear Angel. I peeked at the lake not long ago, and saw that Starlight now has two children. The man she is with seems like a lovely guy, but still..."

"It hurts, I know," Pearl agreed. "I thought you had vowed not to look again? To leave her to live her human life? I know I cannot watch my Flame. It makes me miss him more."

"I had a lapse in willpower recently," Gold said. "I just had to see her face. It feels like millennia since I saw her last. She no longer visits me in her dreams or mediations."

"That's what having two small children will do to you," Pearl said with a chuckle. "It hasn't really been that long, you know. And I am sure it won't be that long before you are reunited again."

"I know, I know," Gold said with a wave of his hand. Pearl wasn't fooled by his flippant dismissal, but she let it go.

"Do you want to go to Earth?" he asked her suddenly. "Despite Aria and Linen no longer being here, running the walk-in programme, it's still possible to go to Earth, you know."

Pearl frowned and considered the Elder's words. Could she really go to Earth? Did she really want to? The longing to feel things in a human way was strong, but her desire to be of service to many souls, and to be connected to the Universe, was stronger.

After a few moments of consideration, she shook her head. "No, I don't think I do. I don't think that walking into someone else's body is the right thing for me right now. Besides, my Flame is of an advanced human age, and will be home soon. So I would hate to leave here and miss his homecoming."

"Fair enough," Gold said. "I just wanted you to know that the option was there. I never want you to feel like you are trapped here, not like me." He chuckled, but Pearl sensed the pain underneath it.

"But you are not trapped here, Gold, can you still not see that? The Indigo Child knows enough, why not go to Earth yourself?"

Gold's eyes were wide as he considered her words. "The intention was for the Indigo Child to take over when I leave for the stars with Starlight. Not to take over for me so I can go to Earth."

"So? What difference does it make?"

"I have not been told of a time I will be on Earth before, Starlight did not mention that in her forecast of the fate of the world."

"I would disagree there, I think there are many world religions that have been prophesying your presence on Earth for millennia."

Gold blushed. "And what a disappointment I would be to them," he said, his tone light, but his face serious.

Pearl shook her head. "Is it any wonder that humans are so full of self-doubt, when you are also?"

Gold smiled. "You are right, my dear Angel." He sighed. "I have not allowed myself the luxury of imagining a life on Earth. It has always seemed so unattainable."

"Aren't you the one always telling souls that anything is possible?"

Gold raised an eyebrow. "I really hate it when my own words are used against me."

Pearl giggled. "Annoying huh?"

"Very."

The two souls became silent then, hearing only the odd wisp of Angelic music and conversation in the distance, drifting to them on the gentle etheric breeze.

"I will think about it," Gold said finally. "I will not make the mistake of saying 'never' because I don't really believe in the word. But right now, I guess I just cannot imagine it."

"Fair enough," Pearl said, echoing his earlier words. "Remain open to the idea. I will also."

Gold nodded. "I must return to my post. I just came to say that there will be an influx of souls soon, and that you may be quite busy. I will be too, which is why I feel I should probably stay."

Pearl sighed. "Man-made or natural?"

"Man-made of course. There is still some way to go before they will learn, I'm afraid."

Pearl nodded. "It would seem so."

Gold hugged her again, then walked away into the mist.

Pearl watched him leave, then began to pray immediately for the souls who would soon be returning home.

CHAPTER THREE

"Hey! Break it up! Back away!"

Without a moment's hesitation, Oscar dove into the fray and managed to avoid the flying fists while he grabbed two wrists and yanked them behind the back of the instigator. His colleague grabbed the victim of the attack and they dragged them away from each other.

Of course, neither were victims, they were both convicted murderers. But it was Oscar's job to ensure that no more murders occurred inside the prison walls.

He marched inmate number 2736 back to his cell, and locked him inside. He would report his behaviour, perhaps he would end up in solitary confinement again. He watched him stalk over to his bunk and throw himself onto it, and Oscar sighed. It really didn't look like he gave a damn.

He headed back to his post, to keep watch on the rest of the inmates while they ate. Scanning the room for any sign of more fights, Oscar's mind wandered a little.

He used to get such a rush from breaking up fights, and dealing with any conflicts that arose in his work. He had joined the army at the age of eighteen, and had served for five years before being discharged after getting shot in the leg in Afghanistan. When he got home, he took the job as a security guard in the prison because his slight limp didn't stop him from doing the job. He had enjoyed it at first, and in comparison to what he had witnessed during his stint in the army, it was easy.

But after a while, it had become boring. The thrill of possible danger no longer gave him an adrenalin rush, and instead, just made him feel tired.

Was he getting old?

He realised that his gaze had stopped on a particular inmate, who was eating alone, trying to be invisible. He had noticed him before. He was a big guy, usually with his head in a book, always on his own, rarely interacting with anyone else.

He wondered what his story was.

"Hey, Oscar, shift's over. See you tomorrow?"

Oscar looked up to see his cover, then glanced at his watch. He had forgotten he was doing a shorter shift that day. He'd promised his son he would attend his rugby game, and had asked for a half day's leave.

He made his way to the staff room, waiting at each check point to be buzzed through. When he finally stepped out into the autumn sunshine, he was yawning. What was happening to him? Why was he so tired?

He opened his car and got in, but before he could turn on the engine, found himself slumping over the wheel and his world going black.

"Oscar? Can you hear me? Oscar, please move your hands or something if you can hear me."

Oscar lifted his head and blinked into a bright light. He frowned. "Sir?"

"What happened? Are you alright?" The light moved away, and Oscar blinked a few times and looked around him. He was still in the prison car park, in his car, but it was now dark.

"One of the guards noticed you were still here, thought you'd left hours ago. Did you pass out?"

Oscar shook his head. "I'm okay," he said, taking stock of his body. "I think I just got overtired, that's all."

His boss didn't look convinced. "So you just fell asleep? Over the steering wheel?"

"Yeah, I guess so." Oscar looked at his watch and groaned. He had completely missed his son's game.

"I should go, see you tomorrow?" Oscar said, switching on the engine.

"No, take tomorrow off. Get some rest. I don't want to see you back until you're one hundred percent again."

Oscar frowned. "I'll be fine, there's no need for a day-"

"I'm not taking no for an answer. Don't come in tomorrow. You're not needed."

Oscar sighed, he really didn't have time to argue. And in all honesty, he really wasn't sure what had actually happened to him. Why had he passed out cold for several hours? Even as tired as he felt, it wasn't like him. "Okay," he relented. "I'll see you in a couple of days."

His boss nodded and stepped back, closing the car door firmly.

On the drive home, Oscar played some loud music, trying to make sure there was no possibility of him falling asleep again. When he pulled into the driveway, he switched off the lights and the engine, then got out of the car, and noticed he felt a little unsteady on his feet. He frowned. Maybe he should actually go get a check-up. Since leaving the army, he had stayed away from doctors as much as possible. He'd had enough of hospitals after his extended stay when he was shot.

He walked up the path to the house, and unlocked the front door to let himself in.

"Where the hell have you been? I called the prison, they said you left hours ago! You missed James' game! You missed dinner! What the hell happened?"

Oscar blinked at the torrent of questions fired at him, feeling them more acutely than the bullets that had been fired at him while in the army. He shook his head at his wife. "I'm sorry, I left work on time, got into the car, and then fell asleep."

His wife frowned. "Fell asleep?" she said, her tone changing as she looked at him more closely. "What do you mean? You fell asleep?"

"I don't know. I remember getting in the car, then the next thing I know, Mick is waking me up, and it's night time."

"Are you serious?"

Oscar sighed at his wife's now ultra-worried tone. "Yes, Ems, but I'm fine now. I think I just got overtired. I'll take it easy tomorrow, Mick is insisting I take the day off."

Emily nodded and then reached out to hug him. He wrapped his arms around her and breathed in the scent of her fruity perfume. "I'm fine, I promise."

He felt her nod, but he knew that it would take more than platitudes to convince her. She had been with him through the tough times he'd had when he'd come back from the war. She was probably reliving some of it in her mind in that moment.

He wouldn't allow himself to relive any of it. He needed to keep it all locked away tight.

He kissed her on the head, then released her and headed to his son's room to apologise for missing the game. He hated the fact that he had let him down. Perhaps he would take him out after school the next day, once he had got plenty of sleep and felt fit again.

*   *   *

"Death?"

Xander smiled at his worried client, as the last card in the spread was turned over.

"Don't worry, the death card doesn't necessarily mean the death of a person. It is a card of transformation, from one form to another. It can mean the end of a relationship and the beginning of a new one, or the end and beginning of careers or even habits, beliefs or ideas. And in this spread, I think it could be pointing toward the relationship. I think the time is coming for a transformation in your relationship with your husband. If it isn't about to end, then I would say that you are about to enter a whole new phase together, that will make your old way of life together look tired in comparison."

His client nodded, looking relieved. Xander looked up to her Guardian Angel stood next to her, and he could see from his expression that the relationship was actually over. He asked him mentally if she would come to realise this soon and he nodded.

"The time of transformation is coming soon, so I would suggest you look at what it is you truly want to do in your life, and that will help you when things shift."

She nodded, and Xander wrapped up their session, bringing it to a close with a silent prayer to the Angels to keep the woman safe. He looked at her Angel again and he nodded, satisfied that she had all the information she needed to move forward.

Xander thanked her, and she made her way to the front of the shop to pay. He picked up the cards and put them back in the deck and gave them a good shuffle. He closed his eyes and cleared the cards, getting them ready for his next client, who he knew would be arriving in less than ten minutes, because their Guardian Angel had already been to visit.

He sat in quiet meditation for a few minutes, then heard voices in the shop. He picked up on a young female voice and knew it was his next client.

"Xander, are you available for another reading? It's four-thirty."

He opened his eyes and looked up at Jackie, the owner of the shop and nodded. He normally finished at this time, but he knew that it was important for him to do this reading.

She left and a few seconds later a woman entered the room, bringing with her the Angel who had visited earlier.

"Please, make yourself comfortable," Xander said, waving at the chair opposite him.

The dark-haired woman sat down, her wide eyes giving away her discomfort as she looked around the dimly lit room.

"I'm Xander, what's your name?"

"Kirsty," she replied.

"Nice to meet you, Kirsty. Have you ever had a reading before?" He already knew from her Angel that she hadn't, but he didn't want to freak her out too much by knowing more than he should.

She shook her head, and he shuffled the deck, then handed them to her. "Just give them a shuffle, then cut them into three piles and reassemble them."

She took the cards from him, and did as requested, and Xander noticed that her hands were shaking a little as she did so. He looked up at her Angel, and asked what the deal was. She shook her head, not giving anything away. Wanted to test his ability to decipher the cards? Okay then, he was up for the challenge.

He decided to do his favourite spread, and took seven cards from the top of the deck and laid them out, He turned them all over, and when he saw the pattern emerge, and the theme become clear, his own eyes widened.

He looked back at Kirsty and studied her features. They did look familiar, could it really be her?

Feeling a little bit shaky himself, he did the reading, and as he spoke, he could see her light becoming brighter and brighter, and the Angel beside her beaming with happiness.

When he finished talking about the meaning of the final card, the lovers, he felt quite emotional.

"Kirsty, why did you come here today?"

She smiled, and her light blue eyes stared into his dark brown eyes. "To find you."

CHAPTER FOUR

Lisa placed the bookmark inside the book and put it down, aware that tears were streaming down her cheeks. She couldn't believe that she was actually one of the characters in Violet's book, or that it explained why she had remained single in this lifetime. It was her guilt over not having healed her soulmate, her husband. She was both protecting and punishing herself. Staying single so that she wouldn't ever have to be in the position of losing someone she loved so deeply again.

She grabbed a tissue from the box on the coffee table, and closed her eyes and sobbed. The memory of that time in the Academy brought with it memories of her previous life, of holding her husband in her arms, of trying at the last moment to give him healing energy, and the crushing guilt of having left it too late.

Her shoulders shook and the pain of the memories ripped through her heart, making her gasp.

She was brought back to the present by her dog, Missy, nudging her hand with her cold nose. She opened her arms and Missy jumped up onto her lap, and she held her close, stroking her coarse, curly fur, and feeling soothed by the presence of her closest friend.

She suddenly realised that though in this lifetime she had been using her healing gifts for good, she still felt an underlying fear that she would be outcast for her abilities, that she would be declared as a witch, and somehow punished for it. She had a very loyal client base, and she loved working at the shop in town, but she knew that if she let go of those fears, she could travel more widely, and even have her own practice, and also charge more for her services. She always felt so guilty, charging people for what she did.

She blew her nose and wiped her eyes, and stared at the cover of Violet's book. How was it possible to have such a strong reaction to what was meant to be a piece of fiction? She had been struggling with these fears and issues her whole life. To have them explained by a story about Angels and Faeries seemed utterly crazy, yet it made complete sense at the same time.

Missy settled on her lap, and she picked the book back up, wanting to know what was going to happen next. She was pleased that she had booked the Sunday off, and had allowed herself to relax and do nothing but read for the day.

Three hours later, she read the last few words of the story, and closed the book, feeling like she had been turned inside out and upside down.

It had been strange reading about Laguz and Velvet, after having seen them in the visions during Violet's healing session earlier in the week. She wondered if Violet had spoken to her Flame about it yet, and about the child they had lost.

She set the book down and stretched her arms above her head, feeling stiff and dehydrated from sitting still for too long. She glanced at the clock and was surprised that Missy hadn't been whining for her food, it was well past her teatime.

She gathered Missy in her arms and stood up, feeling like an old woman as she made her way to the kitchen. She put Missy on the floor, then put the kettle on before picking up the tin bowl and filling it up with dog biscuits. She made herself a cup of tea, then surveyed the cupboards, looking for some inspiration for her own dinner.

She hated cooking for one, she found it utterly tedious. And all of her favourite meals required far too many ingredients and preparation and cooking time to warrant making them for just herself.

She allowed the idea of being in a relationship enter her mind, and immediately she saw herself dancing around the kitchen to the radio, singing into a wooden spoon, while her partner stirred the pot of sauce on the stove so it didn't stick, shaking his head at her antics.

Missy's bark brought her back to her own lonely kitchen and she smiled.

It was time to let go of those feelings of guilt, it was time to forgive herself for what she had done and not done in her many previous lives.

It was time to start afresh.

With that in mind, she decided to make her favourite meal, all the while imagining that she was making it for two, not one.

*   *   *

Considering how much he hated shopping, Quentin was amused to find himself back in the shops the following week after his argument with Jenna. Though there were lots of other things he would rather be doing with his time than fighting the Saturday crowds on the High Street, he wanted to make good on his promise of the best Christmas yet, and he knew that it would require far more than the normal amount of preparation. Jenna was visiting her mother (and thankfully had allowed him to stay home, Jenna's mother hated him and the feeling was mutual) so he thought he would take advantage of the time he had alone to look for presents for her. He wanted to do the whole thing – stocking presents, bigger gifts under the tree, and even a gift on the tree for each of the twelve days after Christmas, so that the fun continued after the big day.

He passed by a jewellers, and then doubled back to look in the window, much to the annoyance of the shoppers walking directly behind him. He looked at the watches, and decided that he needed to get something really nice, that would help her to see how special she was to him. Also, Jenna was always late to everything, which really bugged him. Perhaps if she had a watch, she might be on time.

He went inside, and browsed by himself, happy not to have the attention of the sales people.

"Can I help you at all?"

Quentin sighed, he should have known it wouldn't last. He looked up to say that he was fine, but when he met the eyes of the saleswoman, the words died in his throat. "Um, I'm, um looking for a gift."

She smiled. "Is it for someone special?"

"No," Quentin said, without thinking. Then he shook his head. "I mean, yes, it is. My girlfriend."

"Wonderful, is it a Christmas gift? Have you been together long?"

Despite the intrusiveness of her questions, Quentin found himself unable to resist answering. "Yes it is, and we've been together for seven years."

"I see," the woman said, guiding him over to a cabinet. She pointed out some rings on display. "These are our newest stock of engagement rings, and I think you will agree that they're stunning. And quite affordable too."

Quentin's eyes widened and he looked at the rings, shining and sparkling in the carefully directed spotlight. He gulped and his heart started hammering. Engagement rings? Was that what women expected after seven years? "I was actually thinking of one of those watches in the window," he said weakly, trying to compose himself.

The saleswoman frowned. "Oh I see, I'm sorry, I just assumed that you were looking for a ring."

Quentin shook his head, and breathed a little easier once they moved away from the rings toward the watches.

He chose one of them, which had tiny fake emeralds around the face, (he was sure that Jenna's favourite colour was green) and the saleswoman wrapped it up for him, putting it into a box, then in tissue paper in a tiny gift bag.

"If it's not rude to ask," she said. "Why are you not proposing to her? Seven years is a long time to just be dating."

Feeling a little judged, Quentin found himself puffing out his chest defensively.

"Neither of us are interested in getting married. It's an outdated concept, and besides, our relationship is great. If it ain't broke, why fix it?"

The saleswoman raised an eyebrow but said nothing. "I see." She took the payment, then handed him the gift bag. "I hope she likes the watch, have a wonderful Christmas."

Quentin nodded and took the bag, then left the shop, feeling quite annoyed. Who did she think she was? Questioning his relationship?

And why had she had such an effect on him? When he first saw her, he didn't want to admit he was buying for is girlfriend, because he didn't want her to know he was attached. How awful was that? Did he fancy another woman? Did Jenna really want to get married?

Head whirling, Quentin went into the nearest coffee shop, bought himself an Americano, and sat down.

He thought it would be a simple mission today – find and buy suitable gifts for Jenna, the woman he loved. He hadn't imagined that it would end up with him questioning whether he actually wanted to be with Jenna at all.

He sipped his drink, then winced and added three sugars. He tried to decide whether or not to continue the shopping trip, or to call it a day and go home. He had lost the festive energy that he had started out with, and the idea of fighting the crowds and deciding on things to get Jenna just filled him with dread now.

Quentin finished his drink and took the paper cup to the trash, then left the coffee shop. He was so lost in his thoughts that he was oblivious to the little gift bag that he had left on the bench seat behind him.

CHAPTER FIVE

"What happens when he comes home? Will you still work at the gates, or will you go elsewhere?"

Pearl smiled at the inquisitive Angel. "I will probably get another Angel to take over my post, so that we can be together once more. We may go to the stars, or we may stay here in the Angelic Realm. I will see which he would prefer when he arrives."

"Is he an Angel?" Zoisite asked. "Like you?"

Pearl shook her head. "No, he is an Old Soul, an Elder, in fact, like Gold. Some of the Elders went to Earth to forge the way for the spiritual age to occur. Many of them have returned home already, but my Flame is still there, still teaching, still Awakening Earth Angels and humans." Though Pearl refrained from watching him through the lake, she had an Angel friend who looked out for her Flame for her, and she gave her updates on his journey often. As desperate as Pearl was to see him again, she was so incredibly proud of all the work he was doing on Earth.

"I wish I had met my Flame on Earth," Zoisite said.

"But I missed all the signs that were trying to take me to him."

"Why did you decide to stay then? You were given the option to return to Earth, surely?"

"Of course," Zoisite said. "Gold said I could go back, but, well," she sighed and looked up at Pearl, from her spot on the misty floor. "I was too afraid to return."

"Afraid? What of, my sweet Angel?"

"Being trapped. Of meeting my Flame but not being allowed to be with him. I was born into a culture where your partner was chosen for you. And after seeing how unhappy my parents were, I decided that I didn't want to experience the same fate. Which is why, when the accident happened, and I was asked if I wanted to stay here or return to Earth, I decided to stay."

Pearl nodded. "I can understand your fear. But perhaps you could have spoken to your family, explained that you didn't want an arranged marriage, that you wished to make your own choices. Surely the world has changed enough for that to be possible?"

"In some villages that was happening, but not in ours. I would have had to leave my family and friends and run away to another village, or to the city." She shrugged. "Returning home to the Angelic Realm seemed preferable to doing that. I was far too sensitive to make it on my own in strange places."

"I understand, Angel. We are pleased to have you home, as long as you are happy."

"I am, I guess. Though I still haven't managed to sit and do nothing. I don't think it's a skill I possess. I have decided that I should join the Angelic Assistance Team. There's a few openings, and I think I would be quite good at that."

Pearl smiled. "I think you would be too. They're always looking for extra help. Be prepared to feel frustrated though. Humans often do not listen to the whispers of Angels, they often think they know best, and ignore the warnings we send."

"I know, I think it will be perfect for me to practice having patience with them."

Pearl chuckled. "It will certainly test any patience you do possess. I wish you luck with it."

Sensing that the Angel needed some space, Zoisite rose up off the floor, and hugged her briefly before flying away, toward the part of the lake where the Angels worked tirelessly, trying to keep humans on Earth safe from danger.

"Pearl?"

Pearl turned to see Opalite flying toward her. She landed lightly on her feet a few steps away, then walked to the gates.

"Yes, Opalite? What can I do for you?"

"I have been asked to relieve you of your duty, so that you can attend a meeting with Pallas."

Pearl raised an eyebrow. She had not met with the head of the Guardian Angels for a long time, she wondered why she wanted to see her.

"Now?" she asked.

Opalite nodded. "Yes, if that's agreeable with you."

"Of course," Pearl said. She smiled at Opalite to hide her nervousness, then moved away from the gates, choosing to walk down the path toward the golden building where Pallas ran the Realm. Pearl thought back to the times when Athena had been the head of the Guardian Angels, and how different the energy had been then. As much as she respected

Pallas, she found Athena to be much more approachable.

She reached the ornate golden door, and reached out to turn the handle. She stepped inside and looked around. Though she had been inside many times before, it always awed her, the beauty of the architecture, the shining, glimmering walls and ceilings.

"Pearl," Pallas said warmly, rising up from her chair to greet her.

"Pallas," Pearl replied. "I have been asked to come and see you?"

"Yes, please do make yourself comfortable."

Pearl settled into the soft chair opposite the Angel, and waited for her to enlighten her.

Pallas sat down and sighed. "By now, I had imagined that the world would have evolved more, and that it would be easier than before for the Guardian Angels to guide their charges, and for the Angelic Assistance Team to guide people from potentially dangerous situations. But it seems I was wrong. It is harder than ever to get through to them, to help and assist them."

Pearl nodded, unsure why it concerned her. She waited for Pallas to continue.

"I have decided to put a team together to enter Earth in their own forms, as Starlight did."

Pearl's eyes widened. "You are going to ask a group of Angels to just step onto Earth, in full human form, not walk into an existing human body?"

"Yes. I have spoken with the Elders, and they have agreed to it. These Angels will not suffer from amnesia, they will know who they are, what their mission is, and what they need to do. They will be there to assist humans, and possibly increase their awareness of the existence of Angels. They will be our Earth-based Angelic Assistance Team."

"Is this anything to do with the new influx we are expecting? Gold told me that there will soon be a man-made disaster of some kind, and that many will be joining us soon."

"Partly. If I send my team now, they may be able to save some of those souls, and keep them on Earth so they can complete their mission."

Pearl shifted in her seat, feeling uncomfortable. "I always saw the Angel's place as being a benign, non-judgmental helper, who did not mess with the laws of free will. But what you are going to do, will be to create a team who will have to judge when they should step in and tamper with the free will of humans. Are you sure you can trust that all of the Angels will have the best intentions at heart?"

"There is always a risk that an Angel will fall into ego, and won't be working from their best intentions, but I feel it is worth the risk." Pallas smiled, and Pearl's heart dropped when she realised what was coming next.

"Besides, they will be receiving instructions directly from myself and they will have an excellent team leader. Someone who will not forget the true nature of being an Angel. Someone I trust."

Pearl shook her head. "What if I don't wish to go to Earth? What if I would prefer to stay here?"

"Then I will have to choose someone else to go in your place. But in truth, you are the only Angel that I personally know to be one hundred percent capable of doing the mission properly. I know that nothing will take you off course, and that you will not only save many lives, but you will speed up the process of Awakening in the human race."

Pearl closed her eyes and bowed her head. She knew that the Angel was not deliberately guilting her into going, that she was simply being truthful, but it didn't stop Pearl from feeling guilty regardless.

"Do I have time to decide? Or must you know now?"

"I can grant you time, though I need to send the team as soon as possible. I have already selected the best suited Angels to go, the final team will be of your choosing, should you choose to be the leader."

Pearl nodded. "I shall be back in a few moments with my decision. There is just someone I need to see first."

Pallas nodded and smiled. "I shall see you in a moment then."

Pearl stood and left the golden building, her mind whirling and her heart racing. She flew back to the gates, but didn't stop when she reached Opalite standing at her post. She continued into the mists, seeking out the Elder she knew was waiting beyond.

* * *

"Are you absolutely certain you are back to normal?"

Oscar nodded affirmatively, resisting the urge to salute his boss. "Yes, I have had plenty of rest, some time with my family, and I feel fully capable of doing my work."

Mick sighed. "I would feel better if you had actually gone to see a doctor, but if you feel like you are back to normal, then that's good enough for me. But I want to know if you feel ill again, okay? Don't hide it from me. In this line of work, it could be dangerous."

Oscar nodded then let himself out of the office. He headed to the staff room to drop off his outer clothing. It was getting colder, and though he wasn't a fan of cold weather, he was looking forward to the Christmas holidays. His son still believed in Father Christmas, and he had big plans for this year. He went to his post and put thoughts of his beautiful son out of his mind and shifted into work mode. He had to keep his focus at all times; the inmates could be quite unpredictable and he never knew what might happen.

While keeping watch over the men who were in the lounge area, watching TV and playing board games, he noticed the same quiet inmate reading a book, keeping to himself. He wondered again what his story was, how someone who seemed so quiet and harmless had ended up in the high security prison.

His shift passed uneventfully, which was something of a blessing and a curse. A blessing because he would be going home safely to his family, a curse because it had been incredibly boring and every minute had dragged by.

He was checking the cells later in the evening, before lights out, and he stuck his head in and saw the quiet inmate, sitting on his bed, reading.

"Hey," he said, knowing that interacting with the inmates was not encouraged, but feeling the pull to do it anyway. "Good book?"

The inmate, number 2666 looked up, a frown on his face. He shrugged and tossed the paperback to one side. "Not really. I would prefer to read something with more substance to it, to be honest. Crime and thriller novels aren't really my thing."

Oscar chuckled. "Yeah they're pretty much all the same after a while."

"Definitely. I prefer something with a twist in the tale."

"Me too," Oscar said. He blinked then, and a strange feeling washed over him.

"Hey," 2666 said. "Are you okay?" He stood up from his bed and Oscar tried to focus on his face, but found his vision blurring. He pitched forward and then there was nothing.

"Oscar? Can you hear me? Oscar?"

He could hear his colleague call his name, but he couldn't respond. His head was throbbing and he couldn't quite open his eyes.

"Just stay still, the medic is on their way. Don't move, okay?"

Oscar would have rolled his eyes if he could. Moving wasn't happening right now anyway.

He did an inventory of his body, and found that the only pain was coming from his head. He tried to remember what had happened, and saw the face of inmate 2666 in his head. They had been talking, about... something. It hurt to try and recall anything, all he knew was that he was lying in a very uncomfortable position on the hard cell block floor.

He could hear the flurry of activity that surrounded him, and he wanted to reassure everyone that he was okay, but found he couldn't form the words. He felt someone kneel next to him, and assess the wound on his head. When they touched it, he finally found his voice.

"Shit that hurts!"

"He's coming round," someone said. It sounded like Tony, the medic.

"We'll need a stretcher to get him out of here. I can't see him walking with a head wound like that."

Oscar frowned. Was it really that bad? It didn't feel that serious. But then again, his threshold for pain was pretty high.

It felt like a lifetime, but was probably only a few minutes later when they moved him from the floor to the stretcher. The movement caused the throbbing in his head to increase, and he drifted in and out of consciousness as he was strapped in and an oxygen mask was placed on his face. If the pain in his head hadn't been clouding everything else, he would have felt quite embarrassed by now.

He opened his eyes a couple of times, but the ceiling rushing past made him feel queasy so he kept them shut. Once back in the medical unit, he did his best to respond to the questions, but really just wanted to sleep. The last thing he heard them say before he slipped into oblivion again was that the ambulance was on its way.

CHAPTER SIX

The Christmas music playing in the background was a little distracting, but Xander did his best to tune it out as he listened to Kirsty talking. Since their first meeting a few days before, they had spent as much time together as possible.

"I just can't believe it," Xander said, looking into her clear blue eyes. "I've been dreaming of finding you for so long, it just doesn't feel real."

Kirsty smiled. "I know. There was no reason for me to have a reading the other day, but there was this voice in my head telling me I had to. And for once, I actually listened."

Xander chuckled. "Trouble listening to your intuition? I don't have much choice in the matter, it's too loud and clear to me. And I can't stand the disappointment of the Angels when I don't listen."

Kirsty shook her head. "I can't believe we're sat in a public place, talking about this," she said, looking around the crowded coffee shop. "Don't you find it mad?"

"It seems quite normal to me," Xander said. "It would be mad for me to be talking about ordinary things, to be honest."

Kirsty laughed, and Xander loved the sound of it. "How long have you had the dreams?" she asked, taking a sip of her hot chocolate.

"For the last three years," Xander said. "But you looked slightly different in them. You?"

"Same," Kirsty said with a smile, setting her cup down. "Do you remember our conversations? In the dreams?"

"Some, I have to admit, I never wrote any of them down. I should have, but I didn't realise the significance of it all in the beginning."

"I remember us making plans, to save the world."

Xander chuckled. "Sounds about right. I've always wanted to be a super hero."

"That's because you were one, on the Other Side. You were an Angel. Responsible for saving the lives of many humans over the years."

Xander smiled. "And you were a Faerie, if I remember rightly?"

Kirsty nodded. "Yes. We met at the Earth Angel-"

"Training Academy," Xander finished. "You are the first person I have met on Earth who remembers being there."

"I've met a few, but they were still resistant to accepting it. I must admit, the idea of being part of the Global Awakening feels quite scary to me, too," Kirsty said. "Over the last few months, the feeling has become stronger, that I needed to do something. That I couldn't just carry on with my ordinary life. But the idea of having to do something that would have a big enough impact scared the life out of me."

Xander frowned. "I don't think that we have to do big

things to make a big impact. We just have to do authentic, kind, and loving things. And now we've finally found each other, it should be easy."

Kirsty took in a deep breath and nodded. "I hope so." She finished her drink then glanced at the watch. "Shall we go for a walk? I haven't been to the beach for ages."

Xander nodded and finished his own drink, then stood up and stretched. He took Kirsty's hand in his, and they left the coffee shop.

The walk to the beach was a quiet one, but Xander was acutely aware of all the people they passed, of the colours and shapes and smells of the shop fronts, the items for sale, the bits of music floating about on the breeze. For the last few days, everything seemed like it was in high-definition, with vibrant colours and sounds.

"Doesn't everything seem a little brighter?" Kirsty asked, finally breaking the silence to echo his thoughts, just as they reached the pebbly shore.

"Yes," Xander said. "I was just thinking the same thing."

"If this is what it's like to find a member of your soul family, can you even imagine what it would be like to find your Twin Flame?" Kirsty asked.

Xander squeezed her hand and smiled at her. "I imagine it would be intense. And the connection would be amazing." He sighed. "But sometimes I think that perhaps it would be better not to meet them. To be with a soulmate instead, or someone that I could grow to love over time."

Kirsty frowned, and bent over to pick up a pebble. She straightened up, turning the smooth pebble in her hand, "Why do you say that? Don't you want to meet your Flame?"

Xander looked out to the sea, where the waves were

crashing onto the pebbles, then raking them back. The noise was comforting; he had known it all his life. "The idea of losing control, of losing myself in the embrace of another, it scares me."

"I can understand that," Kirsty said, placing the pebble in his free hand. "But surely the benefits of the relationship would far outweigh the costs?"

"Not according to my readings," Xander said, looking down at her offering. "Every time I have laid out the cards and asked about my Flame, I have seen nothing but destruction and sorrow."

Kirsty leaned into his side and lay her head on his shoulder. "Well, no matter what happens, I'm here now, and I won't let my best friend in the whole Universe go through it alone. We are meant to walk alongside each other, support each other on our missions."

Xander smiled and put the pebble in his pocket. "Yes, we are. And we will."

*　*　*

"You have a full diary today," Ruby said to Lisa as she entered the shop early on the Monday morning.

Lisa nodded and took the sheet of paper from Ruby, then went to the therapy room to get everything set up. She was pleased she'd brought some lunch with her, if the appointments ran over, she might not have enough time to pop out to the shops. She took off her coat and hung it up behind the door, then scanned the names on the list before setting it down. She recognised three of them as regular clients with ongoing problems. Each time she saw them, she tried to peel away another layer, to get to the root cause of their pain and discomfort. She really didn't want them to be reliant on her forever, so she did her best to get her clients to the point where they didn't need to see her, as quickly as possible.

Once the room was ready, Lisa headed back into the shop to chat with Ruby while she waited for her first client. She made them both a cup of tea and settled on one of the chairs behind the counter.

"So," Ruby said. "What did you think?"

"My mind was blown," Lisa admitted. "Did you know I'm a character in the story?"

"No," Ruby said, a smile on her face as she sipped her drink. "But it doesn't surprise me. Which one?"

"One of the second-years. Called Lacy." Lisa shook her head. "It explained everything. Why I've stayed single all this time, why I'm resistant to marketing my healing, why I'm afraid of too many people knowing what I do. It freaked me out a little, I must admit."

"The truth will do that," Ruby said. "I remember reading it for the first time, and thinking – yes, I definitely went there. I remembered it all, exactly as Violet describes."

Lisa looked at Ruby, taking in her appearance and thinking about her personality. "Faerie?" she guessed.

Ruby nodded. "Of course. Fiery, spontaneous, crazy, and mischievous. What else could I possibly be other than an Elemental?"

Lisa giggled. "Can you believe we're having a serious conversation about the fact we're a Faerie and an Old Soul? It seems a little mad."

"I think we're actually the only sane ones here," Ruby

said, as a lady wearing bright pink boots, green tights and an orange dress walked past.

"You may be right," Lisa agreed. The door opened and a blast of cold air swept through the shop, bringing with it a man in a blue raincoat. He pushed his hood down and closed the door behind him, then came over to the counter.

"Hi, Greg," Ruby said. "Here for your session with Lisa?"

"Yes," he said, looking at Lisa with a tentative smile. "Am I late?"

Lisa shook her head, even though he was a few minutes late. "No, you're good. Do you want to follow me?"

Greg nodded and followed her to the therapy room. She put her half-drunk cup of tea down and then held out her hands to take his wet coat from him. He took it off and handed it to her gratefully, and she hung it up behind the door with hers.

She sat down and motioned for him to do the same.

"So, Greg, what can I do for you?"

Greg shifted about in the chair until he was comfortable, then he shrugged. "Um, I don't know. My wife told me I should come and see you."

Lisa smiled. "Fair enough. Well, if you could just fill this out, and then we will do some general healing, if there's nothing specific that you feel you need help with. Is that okay?"

Greg nodded and took the pen and form, then filled out the details in a messy scrawl. He handed it back to her a few minutes later, and she scanned it quickly, just to see if there was anything that jumped out at her.

"Okay why don't you hop up onto the couch, and I'll

just do a general sweep of your body and aura, and we'll see what comes up. If nothing else, it will be deeply relaxing and will hopefully have a calming, restful effect."

"Sounds good," Greg said, getting onto the couch and lying down. "I could do with half an hour of deep relaxation."

He closed his eyes, and Lisa slipped off her shoes and planted her bare feet squarely on the soft rug, bracing herself. Then she held her hands a few inches above Greg's body. She started at the feet, then slowly swept them upwards. When she reached the heart chakra, she felt as though she had tumbled down a wormhole, and when she came out the other end, was in a completely different place.

"She's gone."

Lisa blinked and looked around her. She recognised this house, this was where she had watched Violet with her partner, when they were in Atlantis. She looked to the doorway where Violet stood, her hand on her stomach, her face streaked with tears.

"Our baby's gone," Violet said, barely more than a whisper. Lisa followed her gaze to where Laguz was sat at the table, staring out to sea. He bowed his head, and he seemed unable to move. Lisa's mind was whirling. Greg was Laguz? She hadn't realised. He looked nothing like his previous incarnation.

After what felt like an eternity, Laguz stood up and crossed the room to Violet. Lisa could see the anguish on his face as he took his Flame in his arms.

"I still don't understand," he said. "Why will you not let me carry the burden with you? Why must you bear it all by yourself? Maybe if I could have helped, our child could have surv-"

"There's no way she was going to make it," Violet said, pulling away. "The end of our world will be here long before she would have been born. And I've told you before, I am the only one who can change everyone. I don't know why only I hold this power, but I do know that it is true."

Laguz nodded, the pain still evident on his face. "May I take you to the healer?" he asked, his hand moving to her stomach.

Violet nodded. "I would like that, yes."

A loud noise behind her made her jump, and Lisa found herself being flung out of their world back into her own. She blinked and looked down at Greg, who was looking up at her.

"That's why she wanted me to come here, isn't it? Because of our inability to conceive?"

"You saw that too?" Lisa asked, lowering her arms.

Greg nodded, and rubbed his eyes. He sat up, and Lisa stepped back to sit down in her chair.

"Yes, that's why she came to see me. During her session, I saw the two of you having a conversation about the end of Atlantis, and how she was going to lose your child if she did what she had to, to save everyone."

Greg bowed his head. "She didn't know about the baby we lost, until you told her. She had forgotten. And I had no intention of reminding her."

"Why?" Lisa asked gently.

"Because it's too painful, too raw still."

"For you, or for her?" Lisa asked. "It's been a long time, and you've both had many lifetimes since that happened. It's probably affected all of those lifetimes, for both of you.

Why let it affect this lifetime as well? Isn't it best to heal it, release it, let it go and move on?"

Greg was quiet for a while. "Do you think it can be healed?"

Lisa silently asked her guides the same question, and was a little surprised when she heard the answer. Not wanting to repeat it exactly, she hedged around it. "I don't know."

Greg looked up at her and smiled. "I can hear the 'no' in your voice. And that's okay. Violet and I both have a lot of things we want to accomplish in our lives. If having children is not part of the plan, then I am sure we will find many more ways to make a difference."

"It's not impossible, you know. One day, when the timing is right, it may well happen," Lisa said, wanting to give him some hope.

He nodded. "I'm sure you're right." He hopped off the couch and put his shoes back on, then stood there awkwardly for a moment. "Are we finished?"

Lisa nodded. "Yes, I'm sorry we weren't able to resolve things for you."

"No worries. It was nice to have a relaxing half hour if nothing else."

"Oh, before you go," Lisa said, as he headed for the door. "Could you give Violet this? I read her book, and I would love to chat to her about it, maybe she could give me a call sometime?"

Greg took her business card and nodded. "Sure. I will." He smiled at her then left.

Lisa sighed and sat back in her chair. She felt like she'd been through the wringer. She found it odd that Violet looked the same as she did in her past incarnations, yet

Greg looked nothing like Laguz. She wondered what the story was there.

She heard Ruby and Greg chat for a few moments before she heard the bells on the door ring, as he left. She took in a deep breath and went to the kitchen to get a drink before her next appointment. She needed a moment to gather herself. For some reason, her session with Greg had rattled her a little. She didn't know why, but she intended to meditate on it later when she got home.

CHAPTER SEVEN

"What the hell are you doing here?"

When Quentin saw the sunny smile slip off the face of the pretty saleswoman stood on his doorstep, he regretted his harsh reaction.

She held out a bag to him and he looked down at it, still not comprehending how she knew where he lived.

"You left this at the coffee shop. Someone handed it back to the shop, and I realised it was yours. I found your address on the competition slip you filled out for the Christmas Prize Draw."

Quentin took the little bag and looked inside to see the watch he had bought the Saturday before. He had been in such a daze that he hadn't even noticed that he'd left it behind and come home without it.

"Oh, I see, um, thank you." He looked up at her and she smiled, but it didn't quite reach her eyes. He didn't know what to say to make the situation less awkward, all he knew was that he was having a strange reaction to her presence again.

"Do you want to come in?"

As soon as the question was out of his mouth, he regretted it. Jenna would be home soon, and if she found him home alone with another woman, she would go crazy.

"I'd love that, thank you," she said, stepping inside before he could retract his offer. "It was a crazy day at work, I'm dying for a cuppa."

Quentin nodded and led the way to the kitchen, putting the gift bag down on the kitchen counter. He filled the kettle and got two cups out. "Christmas shoppers driving you mad already?" he asked, at a loss for anything more intelligent to say.

"Yeah, the ones who have no idea what they want are the worst," she said, making herself comfortable at the breakfast bar, kicking off her heels and taking off her jacket.

Quentin set the cup of tea in front of her, and noticed her soft curves through her thin white shirt. She still had her name badge on, which he hadn't noticed when he was in the shop. Probably because he had been purposely trying to maintain eye-contact.

"Delia," he said softly.

"Yes?"

"It's a pretty name."

She smiled and lifted the cup, bringing his attention to her soft lips, and making his heart rate increase. "Thank you."

Quentin turned away and picked up the gift bag from the counter. "I'd better go hide this before my um, uh, Jenna gets home. I won't be a minute.

He went upstairs, wondering why he had stumbled over calling Jenna his girlfriend. He remembered Delia's words in the shop, questioning him on why he didn't want to marry her.

Why didn't he?

While he was upstairs, he decided to slip on more comfortable clothes, he'd not long got home from work and his shirt and trousers were feeling uncomfortable.

Before he could do up his jeans and put a t-shirt on, he heard the front door open.

"Shit," he muttered, grabbing a clean t-shirt from his drawer and running down the stairs. He got to the bottom step just as Jenna was taking her shoes off in the hall. She looked up at him, a smile on her face.

"Jenna's a lucky girl, you make an excellent cup of tea."

Quentin saw the smile vanish from Jenna's face when she heard Delia's voice coming from the kitchen, and she clocked his half-naked appearance. She finished taking her shoes off, then went into the kitchen, with Quentin just a step behind her. He had no idea how to explain the situation, especially as telling her the truth would give away the fact that he had bought her a Christmas present already.

"Hi, I'm Jenna, and you are?"

Quentin heard the poison in her tone and he cringed. He looked at Delia and shook his head wildly. She seemed to pick up on his discomfort, and ignored it completely. She hopped off the stool, her stockinged feet making no sound on the tiled floor. She held out her hand to his girlfriend.

"I'm Delia, lovely to meet you, Jenna. We were just talking about you."

Jenna's rage was almost a palpable cloud around her and Quentin took several deep breaths, while he frantically tried to come up with a suitable explanation, but really, only the truth would do.

"Delia came by to drop off something I left behind while shopping on Saturday," he said, moving to the kettle, hoping to diffuse her anger quickly with her favourite tea.

"You, shopping, Saturday?" Jenna spat, her disbelief evident in every syllable.

Quentin frowned. He knew how unbelievable it sounded, even though it was the truth.

"Yes, I wanted to get a head start on making this Christmas amazing, so I went shopping, I bought a gift, and then then I managed to leave it behind, because I'm an idiot. Delia found it and found my address and delivered it to me."

Jenna was looking from Delia to Quentin, her eyebrow raised in suspicion as she deliberated over the explanation. Delia nodded.

"It's true. I work in the jewellers, he bought the gift, and left it in the coffee shop. Someone handed it back to us and I tracked him down and delivered it. Then I pretty much invited myself in for a cuppa because I was freezing and in need of a hot drink. I hope that's okay."

"You were buying something in the jewellers?" Jenna asked, her face softening and some of the rage visibly dissipating.

Quentin nodded quickly. "Yes. Though it won't be much of a surprise now, sorry."

"No, I'm sorry," Delia said. "I didn't think about that. I shouldn't have said where I worked."

Jenna shook her head. "No, it's okay."

Quentin frowned. It actually sounded as though she meant it. How could it suddenly be okay? Did she really believe him?

"So has it been mad, with all the Christmas shoppers?" Jenna asked Delia, taking a sip of her tea and sitting at the breakfast bar next to her. The two women began to chat as though they were old friends, leaving Quentin feeling quite confused. He looked down and realised he was still half naked, and that he'd dropped the t-shirt on the stairs in his haste.

He went to grab it, and slipped it over his head, then he went into the lounge and put the TV on. He wasn't sure how, but it looked like he'd been let off the hook.

Twenty minutes later, he heard the two women by the front door.

"Bye," Delia called out.

He got up and went to the door, and put his arm around Jenna. "Bye, thanks again, I really appreciate it."

Delia smiled. "Any time." She headed down the path, and down the dark street. Quentin wondered if he should have offered her a lift, but he didn't think he would get away with that. He went back to the lounge and Jenna followed him. They sat on the sofa and she snuggled into his side as her favourite programme came on.

"I love you," she said softly.

"I love you too," he replied automatically, remembering the smile on Delia's face. He tuned out the inane drama playing out on the screen, feeling more confused than ever.

*   *   *

Pearl stood in front of the six Angels she had chosen to assist her on Earth, feeling more nervous than she ever had before in her existence. She still couldn't quite believe that she had agreed to Pallas' request.

"Thank you, brave Angels, for agreeing to join me on Earth. I have absolutely no idea what to expect from this mission, all I know is that we have been afforded the power to enter Earth as we are now, minus the wings, of course," she added with a smile. "And we will be directly assisting humans and Earth Angels in dangerous situations. Though Guardian Angels have the ability to appear and to help their charges at different times, this will be slightly different, as we will be helping on a larger scale. There are some big events coming up, and it will be our mission to save as many souls as we can."

She paused as one of them raised their hand. She nodded for them to speak.

"Why are we being called to interfere in this way? It is not the usual practice for us. What has changed?"

"Humans are listening even less to their intuition and to the whispers of the Angels. For a few years now, it seemed like they were beginning to hear us, they were beginning to heed the still, small voices within. But there is now too much noise. The media is getting louder, the negative voices are getting louder, and it's blocking us out."

The Angel, whose name was Agate, nodded.

"It won't be easy. But we will be liaising with an Angel there who will be able to set us up with provisions while we are human."

"We will need to eat and sleep?"

"Yes, we will need to do everything humans do, except for get jobs and make a living."

"Why don't we have to do that?" Peridot asked.

Pearl smiled. "Because it would get in the way of saving the world." The Angels all chuckled.

"Are we ready? It is time to go."

They all nodded, and Pearl saw Pallas watching from a distance. She lifted her hand to wave to the head of the Guardian Angels, who nodded and smiled in return. Then Pearl led her team to the gates of the Angelic Realm, where she bid Opalite farewell.

"Peace, love and light be with you always," Opalite said softly as the seven Angels walked into the mists.

"And with you," Pearl replied.

When the mists swallowed them up, Pearl took a deep breath and held her hand out to Peridot who took it, and then took hold of Agate's hand.

Pearl whispered. "We're ready."

Within a second, she opened her eyes and saw that they were stood, a chain of seven Angels, on a hill overlooking a town.

She looked over at her team. "We're here. Let's get to our destination before nightfall. We have a lot of planning to do."

The other Angels agreed, and they all fell into line as they walked down the hill. In the transition, their wings had disappeared and their robes had changed into ordinary human clothing, suitable for the terrain they were now hiking down. Having a human body, and no wings, felt alien to Pearl. By the time they reached the bottom of the hill, she found herself breathing quite hard. She looked at the red cheeks and sweaty foreheads of her fellow Angels, and knew they were feeling the same way.

They walked through the streets, and Pearl felt as though

her eyes were as wide as saucers as she took in the sights and sounds and smells. It was such a different experience, to actually be on Earth, rather than to just view it from the Angelic Realm.

When they reached the house that Pearl had seen in the lake, she stopped and knocked on the door.

Moments later, the door opened, and a confused man stood there, a frown on his face when he saw the seven bedraggled Angels, masquerading as hikers.

"Yes?"

"Is Sarah there?" Pearl asked.

He nodded, but the frown remained. "Sarah!" he called over his shoulder. "It's for you."

A moment later, a woman with long blonde hair appeared, with two children in pyjamas following behind her.

Her eyes widened when she saw Pearl, who smiled.

"Hello there," she said softly to the Angel of Destiny.

"Pearl!" Sarah said, throwing her arms around the sweaty Angel. "Oh my goodness! I can't believe you're here!"

"I'll get the kettle on I guess," the man said, moving away from the door, taking the kids with him.

Pearl pulled back to look into Sarah's eyes.

"It's so good to see you, Starlight," she said.

CHAPTER EIGHT

"I have epilepsy?"

Oscar stared at the doctor in disbelief, who was nodding. "I'm afraid so. These blackouts you've been experiencing are actually severe fits. We need to do some more tests to confirm that there isn't anything more serious going on."

"More serious than epilepsy?" Oscar asked, feeling sick.

"For epilepsy to start as suddenly as this indicates that there could be another underlying issue. It would be good to rule that out."

Oscar nodded, wishing that his wife were there with him, but she was getting James off to school before coming in to see him. "Thank you, Doctor. So how long do I have to stay in?"

"A few more days to give us time to observe you, do more tests and then work out what medication would be best to keep it under control."

Oscar nodded, but needed to know one more thing. "Will I be able to return to work?"

The doctor shook his head. "Considering the line of

work you are in, and the situation you got yourself into, I wouldn't recommend that you return, no. It could be too dangerous."

Oscar's heart sank, and his mind whirled. How was he going to support his family if he couldn't work? What other employer would take him on, knowing that he could have a fit and pass out at any moment? He pulled himself out of his thoughts long enough to thank the doctor, who left to continue his rounds, then he sank back into the pillows and into the black hole of his thoughts again.

Luckily, a few minutes later, a nurse brightened the mood with a breakfast tray. She set it in front of him and fussed over him, plumping up his pillows and putting the bed into a more upright position.

He smiled his thanks and then reached for the pot of yoghurt, pulling the lid off slowly. What kind of work could an ex-army officer, ex-prison guard do, that wasn't physical in nature?

"Morning, sweetheart."

Oscar blinked and looked up to see his wife entering the room, a brown paper bag in her hand. She set it down on his breakfast tray and he set aside the half-eaten yoghurt and reached inside the bag eagerly. He'd know that smell anywhere.

"Thought you'd appreciate your favourite bacon sandwich from Jimmy's," she said, kissing him on the forehead.

"Thanks, this is great," he said, unwrapping the greasy offering and tucking in. After two bites he closed his eyes and sighed in appreciation. It had just the right amount of brown sauce on it.

"So have you seen the doctor yet? Have they figured out what's going on?" she asked as she gently touched the bandage on his head. "Does it still hurt?"

He swallowed his mouthful, wishing that he could have had a little more time to enjoy his favourite breakfast before being barraged with questions, but he knew that she had probably spent all night worrying about him, so he couldn't feel too upset about it.

"Doc says I have epilepsy. They need to do more tests to see what might be causing it."

"Epilepsy? Are you serious?" she asked, her eyes wide. "How is that possible? People don't just get epilepsy out of the blue."

Oscar shrugged and bit into the sandwich again. He closed his eyes and savoured the taste of the crispy bacon on his tongue.

"How long are they keeping you in?"

"A few more days," Oscar said, his mouth still full.

His wife nodded and sat down on the chair next to him, looking as shocked as he'd felt by the diagnosis.

"I guess we just have to wait then."

"Yeah," Oscar said. "Was James okay this morning?"

"Yes, he was fine. Mum's picking him up after school, so I can stay here with you. He wanted to come and see you, but you know how much he hates hospitals."

"Him and me both," Oscar said.

His wife dug around in her over-sized handbag and pulled out a dog-eared book. "I brought your novel, in case you wanted to read it." She handed it to him, and then dug out her own book, flicked to the bookmark and settled back into the chair to read.

Oscar finished his sandwich then turned to the next chapter in the novel, making himself focus on the words on the page.

It was going to be a long day.

*   *   *

"That really suits you, you know. You should buy it."

Kirsty turned around slowly, checking out the dress from every angle in the mirror, and shook her head at Xander. "I think it makes me look fat," she said.

Xander laughed. "On what planet could anything make you look fat?" He got up from where he sat on the shop sofa and came up behind her. He placed his hands on her slim hips. "You look amazing. Now buy it. You could wear it for the Christmas party I'm going to have at my place."

Kirsty turned and smiled at him. "You're having a party? I love parties! Okay, fine," she turned to scrutinise her reflection for a few moments longer. "I'll get it. But I'll have to lay off the mince pies until the party, or I won't fit into it."

Xander shook his head to himself, and sat back down again while she went to change back into her own clothes. He couldn't believe how low her self-esteem was, could she really not see just how beautiful she was? It seemed utterly ridiculous to him. He felt his phone buzz in his pocket, and he pulled it out and woke it up. A text message from his mum popped up, and he scanned it quickly.

He sighed. She was asking him to go home for Christmas. He put his phone back in his pocket without replying. The idea of having to sit through another family Christmas dinner turned his stomach. Having to listen to how perfect his siblings were, how much money they were making, how beautiful their children were – ugh. They never asked him about his life or his work, because they were ashamed of the fact that their youngest son had become a tarot reader who could see and speak to Angels.

Kirsty came out of the changing cubicle, with the dress in her hand. She smiled at Xander then headed for the counter to pay for it.

Xander got up and joined her there, and when she pulled her purse out, he put his hand out to stop her and handed his card to the assistant instead.

"I insisted you get it, so I insist it's on me," he said, loving how her whole face lit up at his words.

"Oh, Xander, you don't have to do that! I can get it."

"Nope," Xander said, tapping in his pin number. "Too late now."

Kirsty beamed at him the whole time the dress was being carefully packaged and slipped into a paper bag. She accepted it from the assistant and thanked him, then she tucked her arm into Xander's as they left the shop.

"You would make the perfect boyfriend, you know," she said. "You're patient while I'm shopping, you tell me I look amazing, even though I look a little chubby, and then you pick up the bill." She grinned sideways at him as they made their way to their favourite coffee shop. "Keep going like this, and I might just be forced to ask you out."

Xander chuckled, but inside he felt a fluttering in his stomach. He glanced at the beautiful woman walking beside him, and the idea of being more than just friends with her didn't seem ridiculous.

They reached the coffee shop, and he held open the door for her, then went to the counter to order them both their favourites while she snagged their usual table.

"You two make such a sweet couple."

Xander looked up at the barista, and frowned. "Excuse me?"

"I'm sorry, it's just that the two of you come in here so often, and I've noticed that you just look really good together, there's an almost tangible energy around you both." She shrugged, looking uncomfortable. She finished his order and placed it all on a tray, then took his payment.

"We're not together," Xander said slowly, trying to process why the Universe was trying to tell him that they should be. "We're best friends."

"Oh," the barista said, a blush appearing on her cheeks. "I'm sorry, I just assumed, please ignore what I said."

Xander smiled and put his change in the tip jar before picking up the tray. "Don't worry about it, it's cool."

He joined Kirsty at their table, a puzzled smile still on his face.

"What is it?"

He looked at his friend, his mind whirring like crazy. He told her what the barista had said and Kirsty shrugged.

"We do make a good couple, nothing weird about that."

Xander sipped his coffee, then set it down and reached over to touch her hand. "Do you think we should be together?"

Their eyes met and he saw that she was thinking hard about his words.

"I still want to meet my Twin Flame," she said softly. "I'm sure he's out there, somewhere, and I want that connection with him."

Xander nodded and pulled his hand away. But before he could pick up his cup again, she continued.

"But, I do love you."

Xander's eyes widened and he looked into her eyes, seeing the truth in them. "I love you too," he admitted. "You're my best friend, I feel like I could tell you anything. I can see how beautiful you are, and it kills me that you can't see it too."

Kirsty smiled and reached out to take his hand. "So what do we do now? I don't want anything to happen to our friendship, it's the best thing in my life right now, but I can't ignore the fact that we are amazing together."

Xander blinked, and suddenly he became aware of her Guardian Angel sitting next to her, grinning at him. He silently asked the Angel if they were meant to be together in a relationship, and the Angel nodded and smiled at him.

He refocused on Kirsty, who was sipping her tea and patiently waiting for an answer. She was used to him drifting off every now and then as he conversed with spirit.

"I say we should go for it," he said, squeezing her hand. "But I vote that no matter what happens, we always remain friends."

"Deal," Kirsty said. She leaned toward him across the table and closed her eyes. His heart beating furiously, he leaned forward to meet her and the moment before his lips met hers, he closed his eyes.

CHAPTER NINE

"Lisa! Come on in."

Lisa stepped into the warm and inviting front room, and smiled at Violet who held her arms out to hug her. They embraced for a few moments, and Lisa felt her nervousness recede a little.

"Thank you for inviting me to dinner, I really appreciate it. I must admit, making meals for one is not my favourite thing to do."

Violet took her coat from her and hung it up, and offered her some house slippers to wear. "You're so welcome, we love having people for dinner, gives Greg an excuse to be more adventurous in the kitchen. My friend Julie is here as well, I hope that's okay."

Lisa's heart sank a little that she might not get a chance to have a word privately with Violet, but she smiled and nodded to cover her disappointment. "Of course, that's great."

She followed Violet through to the lounge, and then to the kitchen beyond where Greg was cooking and chatting to a lady who was sat on a stool, drinking mulled wine.

"Hi!" she said, when Lisa entered. "I'm Julie," she held out her hand and Lisa shook it.

"Lisa," she said. "Nice to meet you, Julie."

"Mulled wine?" Julie asked. When Lisa nodded, Julie hopped off the stool and went to the stove where a large pan was simmering. She ladled the wine into a cup and then handed it to Lisa. The smell of it immediately brought back a thousand memories of previous Christmases, and Lisa smiled.

She settled on a stool next to Julie, while Violet joined Greg in making the dinner.

"So you're a healer?" Julie asked. "Violet said both she and Greg have been to see you."

"Yes," Lisa said. "I work out of the crystal shop in town."

"Are you making a living from it, or would you like to be getting more business?"

Lisa's eyes widened at her forthright questions, but before she could feel defensive, she realised that she had been thinking just the other day that she needed to expand her practice, and be more confident in her abilities. She decided to be honest.

"Not a very good living," Lisa admitted. "And yes, I would love to expand it. Is that something you can help me do?"

"I knew you two would get on," Violet said from across the kitchen as she grated some cheese.

Julie laughed. "And you were right. I swear you should get commission for all the connections you help people to make."

Violet giggled. "Sounds good to me." She waved her

hand. "Keep talking, I won't butt in again."

Julie turned to Lisa, who was sipping her mulled wine. "Yes, I can help you with that. It's my mission on this planet to help Earth Angels who are following their missions to be able to make a living from their passions. And if you are as good as Violet says you are, then there's absolutely no reason why you shouldn't be making a great living for yourself."

Lisa blushed and looked up at Violet. "I don't know what Violet has said, but I'm sure there are better healers out there than me."

"You are amazing," Violet said. "I've been to a lot of healers over the years, and none of the others have gone straight to the source of the problem as quickly and easily as you did."

Lisa smiled, and saw the look that Greg and Violet shared, and wondered if they had talked to one another about the conception issue. Despite her need to downplay her abilities, she knew that it was the perfect moment to tell them about the vision she'd had when she explored their life in Atlantis further. But she was hesitant to bring it up in front of Julie, because she didn't know how close a friend she was, and how much she knew.

"Remind me later, to tell you something interesting that came up in a meditation after Greg's healing session," she said, hoping that the hint would make Violet curious enough to get them some time on their own later.

"Ooh, what was it?" Violet waved a hand at Julie. "You can say it in front of Julie, she's one of my closest friends. She was a professor at the Academy too, so we go way back."

Lisa looked at Julie. "Wow, which professor?"

"Cotton, Professor of Patience," Julie replied. "I didn't realise until I read Violet's book though."

"That's really cool. One of the reasons I wanted to chat to Violet again is because I read the book, and I recognised myself in it too."

"You did?" Violet said, drying her hands on a tea-towel and joining the two ladies while Greg continued cooking. "Who were you?"

"Lacy, Old Soul and Second Year trainee."

Violet's eyes widened. "The one who lost her husband in her previous life because she was too afraid to heal him? In case she was outcast?"

Lisa's eyes filled with tears and the pain of losing her husband in that life came flooding through her body. "Yes," she said, pulling out a tissue from her pocket and blowing her nose.

Violet reached across and squeezed her arm gently. "No wonder you're finding it difficult to be more open about your healing abilities."

Lisa nodded. "I know that I decided to release those fears before I started this life, but it feels as though the echoes of them still have a hold over me."

"Greg might be able to help you there, he's very good at helping souls to release old emotional baggage," Violet said. "There's really no need for you to be afraid to shine as a healer. You really are good. So what was in the meditation?"

Lisa took a deep breath, ignoring her inner voice that was screaming at her to shut up and keep playing small. "I wondered why seeing yours and Greg's lives in Atlantis affected me so deeply, and so I did my own meditation where I visited those times. I found that I was there too, at the same time. I was the healer that you visited when…" her voice trailed off when she saw Greg shake his head at her from behind Violet. "When you were sick," she finished vaguely.

"You were our healer in Atlantis? Really?"

"Yes, and I was one of the ones who left for the seas, I remember you changing me into a Merperson."

"Wow," Violet said, her eyes wide. "That's so crazy. What are the chances of you being our healer during Atlantis, and now being our healer in this life too? Did you realise that Atlantis was the last human life Greg and I had together before this one?"

"No, I didn't."

Violet glanced up at Greg. "Yes, we were apart for a very long time."

Lisa heard the pain in Violet voice, and wondered what it would feel like to love that deeply. Though she had really loved the husband she'd lost, he was not her Flame, and she knew it was a different kind of connection.

"It's funny to think that if someone who knew nothing of Earth Angels and Twin Flames heard this conversation, they would think we were all completely crazy and have us locked up," Julie joked, drinking the last of her mulled wine.

Violet and Lisa giggled, and the atmosphere in the kitchen lightened up. "True," Violet said. "I've half expected to be carted off to a mental institution for the last few years. But I think the fact that we haven't been sectioned is a sign that the world really is waking up."

"Yes, though I always imagined that by now, the world would be a little more Awake than it actually is," Lisa said.

"Food's ready," Greg said, interrupting them. They all helped to take the food through to the dining table, then settled down while Greg served and Violet topped up their wine.

"Are you trying to get us all drunk?" Lisa asked. "I won't be able to drive soon."

"No worries, just stay in a pod. Julie is staying, and we haven't any other guests tonight."

"We're having a brainstorming session tomorrow, to see how we can get this place more fully booked up," Julie said, tucking into her food immediately. "You could brainstorm with us, then we could brainstorm ideas for your healing business too."

Lisa sipped her wine and nodded. She was sure that if she texted her neighbour, he would let Missy out into the garden for a bit tonight and then again in the morning. He often did when Lisa was visiting her family. The idea of staying over and spending more time with Violet and Julie was too tempting to miss.

"Sounds great, I'm in," she said, raising a glass to her new friends.

"To new ideas, and expanding businesses," Julie said clinking her glass against Lisa's.

"To finding old friends again," Violet said with a smile, clinking her glass against theirs. They all looked at Greg, who then raised his glass.

"To eating food while it's still hot."

The three women giggled, and without another word, all tucked into the meal Greg had cooked.

* * *

Jenna's behaviour continued to flummox Quentin, and he wanted to ask her what was going on, but didn't want to get into an argument, so he just continued as normal, going to work, watching TV, and going to the pub with his friend on a Friday night.

It was after a drinking session that he got home and could hear Jenna chatting on the phone in the kitchen. He wasn't trying to sneak around, but it was clear that Jenna hadn't heard him enter the house, because she didn't lower her voice as he approached the kitchen.

"It's really happening, I can't believe it," Jenna said, the excitement in her voice obvious. Quentin paused in the hallway, the alcohol taking away any feelings of guilt he may have had for eavesdropping.

"I know, it is about time too. I hope he does it on Christmas Day, I don't think I could wait until New Year's."

Quentin frowned. She hoped he would do what?

"No, I had no idea, I mean, whenever the subject has come up, we've both said we're not bothered, but it doesn't mean that I wouldn't jump at the chance. And as it turns out, Quentin must feel the same way too."

Thoroughly confused now, Quentin gripped onto the door frame and strained to hear the rest of Jenna's words.

"Of course you'll be my maid of honour! You're my oldest friend, how could you think I would ask anyone else?"

In that second, everything slotted into place and Quentin suddenly felt sick.

Jenna thought that the gift he'd bought from the jewellers was an engagement ring. And that he was going to propose at Christmas. A wave of nausea washed over him, and he wondered if he would actually throw up.

He slowly made his way back to the front door, opened it and then slammed it hard, to announce his arrival home. He headed to the kitchen and heard Jenna wrapping up the conversation with her best friend.

"Hey, babe," Jenna said, hanging up the phone and coming over to him. She recoiled a little at the sight of him, and the smell of beer on his breath. "How many did you have? I thought you said you were only going to have a couple?"

Her nagging voice registered through his drunken haze, and mixed with the uneasiness in his stomach. He only had enough time to dash to the kitchen sink before he unleashed his dinner and the kebab he'd had on the way home.

"Oh, that's just disgusting," Jenna complained loudly over his retching.

He turned the tap on, and washed his vomit down the over-sized plughole, then switched on the waste disposal unit to get rid of it. He grabbed a glass and poured himself some water.

"Have a shower before you come to bed, I won't be able to sleep with that smell otherwise."

There wasn't a scrap of sympathy in her voice, and Quentin didn't even look up as she left. He turned around and leaned against the counter, his poor, drunk, muddled brain trying to process everything, and not getting very far.

He sipped the water slowly, and tried to figure out what to do. Considering the fact that hearing Jenna talking about him proposing to her made him vomit, he realised that he didn't want to marry her.

In which case, why was he still with her?

He thought of Delia, and his stomach flipped, though this time in a pleasant way. She'd popped up in his thoughts regularly since the day she'd come over with the watch, and he'd resisted going to the town centre and seeing her in the jewellers, but if he was honest with himself, he was tired of resisting it. He wanted to see her again.

He finished his water and set the glass down. There was no need to try and make any big decisions straight away, he would get some sleep and wait until the alcohol was out of his system before making a decision that would affect the rest of his life.

He had intended to go upstairs, shower as instructed and get into bed, but he got as far as the living room and decided that the couch was a much better idea, and collapsed onto it.

Within moments, he was out cold.

CHAPTER TEN

"Is everyone ready?"

Pearl looked around the faces of her team, some of whom looked a little scared, and they all nodded except for one.

"I'm still unsure as to why we need to cause an accident in order to save these people. Why can't we just create a roadblock, or go to the police and insist they stop people from going near the area, because if they do, they'll die?"

Pearl looked at Galena and smiled. "You know that humans have trouble heeding words of caution if they cannot see the danger. Causing this accident will ensure that they are caught up in the drama and then later, they will see that the drama actually saved them from being involved in a bigger catastrophe."

"Galena's right though," Pietersite argued. "Why can't we just stop the catastrophe? Why let it happen at all?"

"Because the events that will create it are already in motion, we cannot change it. But we can limit the number of souls who will go home as a result of it."

She looked around her team, who were all looking a little uncomfortable. "What is it?" she asked softly.

The quietest member, Larimar, spoke up. "We still don't quite understand the point of this whole mission. Back on the Other Side, it seemed like a good idea, like a noble idea, but now that we're on Earth, we struggle to see the point of it. After all, why is it such a bad thing for souls to go home, if it's their time? Should we really be tampering with their free will in this way?"

Pearl nodded. "I feared this would be an issue, I had the same problem when Pallas first asked me to do this. After speaking with my dear friend, Gold, I have come to realise that we do not need to understand it, we only need to act. If it is indeed time for those souls to leave Earth, they will leave some other way regardless of what we do. But it is my understanding that if we save these souls, it will set in motion a wave of energy that will help the world to Awaken. And that our presence here will spark something, and create something magical. Not all of our deeds will be huge, sometimes, we will simply be acknowledging the existence of humans who may be on the verge of giving up. Sometimes we will just be smiling, doing acts of kindness or helping a person out. But today, we are going to do this, and save at least fifty lives. Are you with me?"

There were six nods this time, and so Pearl led the Angels from Sarah's living room, to the cars outside that Sarah had arranged for them. Pearl, Peridot and Agate got into one vehicle, Smithsonite and Pietersite got into the second, and Larimar and Galena got into the third.

Pearl took a deep breath, then started the engine. Though she had the knowledge of driving a car, actually driving one was a different thing altogether. She didn't think it would be difficult to cause an accident with their non-existent driving experience.

She tried to keep her mind on the road and the task at hand. But as they made their way to the motorway, Pearl's mind wandered to the instructions she'd received from Pallas. If she was honest, she didn't really understand it either. Surely causing an accident held the possibility of harming people? And what would happen if she or any of her team were harmed? She supposed they would just 'die' and then they could come back again. But if they went to the hospital, and to the morgue, they would be found to have no human ID, and that might cause problems.

"Pearl?"

She glanced at the passenger seat where Agate sat. "What?"

"Everything will work out just fine. None of us will be harmed, and no humans will be harmed either. I can see it."

Pearl nodded. She knew there was a reason why she had chosen Agate for the team. He was the most stable, grounded Angel she had ever met, and he had a wonderful calming influence on her.

"Thank you, I appreciate that."

"We're nearly there," Peridot spoke up from the back seat.

Pearl nodded, she recognised the turning from the instructions she'd been given.

"Okay, Angels, this is it. Let's go save lives." She looked in her rear view mirror and saw the two cars with the rest of the team in follow her onto the motorway. After a few minutes, she saw the signs that indicated the right spot, and she glanced around, relieved to see there weren't any other cars too close, other than the Angels following her. She took a deep breath, prayed silently that it wouldn't hurt, and then swerved the car to the right with a violent jerk of her hand, while simultaneously slamming on the brakes, causing the car to skid around in a circle.

Before the car could come to a stop, the car directly behind them slammed into their side, making Pearl's head hit the side window, and Peridot scream.

When the third car hit, with Larimar and Galena in it, Pearl was jolted from nearly slipping into unconsciousness, and saw their car flip over and land on its roof. She blinked and groaned. Had they been going too fast? She was sure that the accident wasn't meant to be quite so severe.

She breathed deeply, raised her hand to her head, and rubbed the tender spot. She was almost surprised to see that she wasn't bleeding.

"Everyone okay?" she asked her passengers. She looked around to see Peridot and Agate nodding, though both looking a little ashen. "Let's go help the others. Remember your story, for when the police turn up, okay? An animal darted out into the road and I was trying to avoid it."

They slowly got out of the car, and Pearl's head was throbbing with every movement. She and Peridot went over to the overturned car, and Agate went to assist the car embedded in the side of theirs. Pearl glanced past the carnage and saw that all of the traffic after them had come to a standstill, and people were beginning to get out of their cars to investigate.

She reached the overturned car and knelt down on the glass-covered tarmac, glad that she had worn jeans that day. She peered into the front of the car, where Larimar and Galena were suspended upside down, their seat-belts holding them in place.

"Are you okay?" she called out. They were both conscious, and they turned to look at her.

"I think so," Galena, who was in the passenger seat, said. "Beginning to feel quite uncomfortable now though."

"Let's get you out then," Pearl said. "Can you undo your seatbelt? I can find something to put under your head to break your fall."

"Yes, I can reach the seatbelt clips. Something soft would be nice."

Pearl straightened up a little and pulled off the thick, padded jacket she was wearing, and folded it up tightly. She was aware of sirens in the distance, and of people gathering, but she focused on freeing her team.

She put the jacket under Galena's head, and encouraged her to undo her seatbelt, and as slowly as she could, ease herself down. It was a little bit awkward, but she managed it without too much trouble. Pearl helped her to slide sideways out of the broken window, trying to take care not to cause cuts and scrapes. Then she joined Peridot on the other side of the car, where she was helping Larimar out. Pearl glanced over to the other car to see both Smithsonite and Pietersite standing beside the wreck they'd been driving only a few minutes previously, and breathed a sigh of relief. It appeared that her team had escaped unscathed and her nightmare scenarios of Jane or John Does and morgues were unfounded.

The police and fire engines arrived on the scene about five minutes later, and Pearl made sure that they didn't hurry to answer their questions. She glanced at her watch. They needed to continue blocking the road for at least another ten minutes for it to be effective, and for their mission to be a success.

"How did this happen?" she was asked for the third time.

"There was an animal, it was too fast to see what it was; I swerved to avoid it and lost control of the car."

The office nodded, appearing to accept her story without question. Probably because Agate and Peridot had already confirmed the same thing.

Two ambulances arrived, and the paramedics fussed over the seven of them, checking for any injuries, they seemed surprised to find none. It took a little convincing that they didn't need to go to the hospital, and after giving false details to the police and to each other, Pearl glanced at her watch, and glanced up at the car park they had created. She watched the seconds tick down, and then a loud boom reverberated through the air, making everyone turn around and a few people shriek in surprise. Pearl turned just in time to see the cloud of smoke and the flames shooting up from the industrial estate next to the motorway. She had been told that without the road block, the explosion and the black smoke would have caused a huge pile up, and killed at least fifty people. She glanced at the opposite side of the motorway, but the smoke wasn't quite obliterating the road, and motorists were already slowing down and being more cautious.

The police and firemen came out of their apparent trance and sprang into action, jumping into their vehicles and speeding toward the off-ramp leading to the building that was now ablaze.

Pearl had been told that their 'accident' would ensure that there were plenty of emergency vehicles in the vicinity, thereby making sure that as many people were saved from the blaze as possible.

She looked across to Galena, who was nodding. She could see the synchronicities that their intervention had created, and seemed to understand now why it had been necessary.

Pearl realised that the throbbing in her head had subsided. It seemed that despite being on Earth in human form, injuries didn't take hold.

"I wonder what we'll have to do next," Smithsonite said, looking excited at the prospect. "I have to admit, that was a lot of fun."

Pearl glanced about to make sure that no one was close enough to hear and she smiled at him. "It's the most action I've ever seen in my existence, that's for sure."

Peridot chuckled. "From standing at the pearly gates to causing RTAs. Whatever next?"

"I guess we'll have to wait and see."

*   *   *

"Oscar! Wasn't expecting to see you back so soon, how's the head?"

Oscar touched the side of his head, which was still tender, and shrugged. "It'll heal. Unfortunately, I'm not here to come back to work. I came to speak with you."

Mick frowned. "I don't think I like the sound of this," he said, leaning back in his chair.

"It seems I have epilepsy. When I blacked out in the car, and in the cell last week, I was actually having a fit."

Mick's frown deepened, and as well as concern, there was something else in his expression that Oscar couldn't read.

"Shit, that doesn't sound good. What does it mean? Can they treat it?"

"Yes, there are drugs and treatments, but the doctor has said that it's too dangerous for me to work in this kind of environment anymore, because if I had a fit again, and I wasn't found quickly, anything could happen."

"As much as I hate to say it, I think I agree with the Doc there. I don't think my insurance will cover staff with medical conditions that make them vulnerable. So you've come here to resign?"

Oscar shrugged. "I don't have much choice."

"You might do, let me check out what other positions we have that have no prisoner contact, and if nothing grabs you, then I will happily make you redundant. At least that way, you'll get some pay out from it."

Oscar smiled and felt a huge amount of relief. He'd been afraid that Mick would react badly to the news, but he was actually being incredibly generous.

"That sounds amazing. Is it okay if I just say hi to couple of buddies before leaving?"

"Sure," Mick, said, looking a little uncomfortable. "I'll drop you a line about positions, okay?"

Oscar nodded, and got up and let himself out of the office.

He made his way through the building, and got buzzed through each checkpoint until he reached the lounge area where his colleagues were on duty.

"Hey," he said as he entered. "Have they been behaving while I was gone?"

"Oscar! Are you back? Are you better? How's the head?"

"It's alright, but I'm afraid I won't be back, I've got epilepsy."

"Epilepsy?" Jason's eyebrows shot to his hairline. "You mean you were having a fit?"

"Yep, I wanted to apologise to 2666, I must have freaked him out completely."

"Um, yeah, um, well," Jason shifted from foot to foot and looked down at the floor, reminding Oscar of Mick's behaviour.

"What's going on? What happened after I blacked out? Everyone is acting really shifty."

Jason sighed. "Well you can imagine how it looked? You were out cold on the floor, head bleeding like you wouldn't believe, and 2666 was standing over you, blood on his hands, screaming. They thought, well, they thought he did it."

Oscar frowned. "Did what?"

"He's in for murder. Killed his girlfriend's dad with his bare hands," Jason said in a hushed voice. "We thought he'd tried to kill you, too. He was completely incoherent, making no sense. So he was put in solitary for a week. And it's on his record now, that he assaulted you."

Oscar's eyes were wide as he digested this information. "I never thought I'd say this, but fuck! Poor guy! He didn't do anything. In fact, he probably saved my life. I must have hit my head on something when I went down, and his screaming and stemming the blood saved me. Where is he now? I need to see him, I need to apologise."

"He's in his cell. You'll need supervision, because it's on record now, they won't leave you alone with him."

Oscar nodded, and waited for Jason to request cover for his post so he could come with him to visit inmate 2666. Oscar couldn't believe that they'd thought he'd attacked him, why hadn't anyone said anything? Why hadn't they asked him? To just punish him, and further tarnish his record seemed extreme, even if he was a convicted murderer.

They reached the cell, and Jason opened the door and both he and Oscar stepped inside. 2666 was lying on his bed, reading the same book that he'd been reading the previous week. He looked over at them when he heard the door, and when he saw Oscar, he set the book down and sat up slowly.

"How are you?" he asked, looking genuinely concerned.

Oscar nodded. "I'm fine, my head will heal. I wanted to apologise for how you were accused of attacking me, and for them punishing you. I know you didn't do anything, I had an epileptic fit."

2666 nodded. "You hit your head on the door-frame," he said. "I tried to stop you from hurting yourself but wasn't quick enough." He looked down. "The sight of the blood triggered bad memories, so I couldn't actually do anything other than yell to get attention. I couldn't explain what had happened." He looked up. "It's not your fault they punished me. It was an easy conclusion to come to, considering my conviction."

Oscar nodded. "I appreciate you being so decent about it, but I am really sorry. I will make a statement to the prison that you were trying to help me, and that you didn't attack me, hopefully the incident will be taken off your record, otherwise it might affect your chances of parole."

The inmate shrugged. "I'm in here for a good while yet anyway. Got used to it now." He glanced up at a photograph on the wall, and Oscar moved a little closer to see the image, aware that Jason was just a step behind him.

"She's beautiful," he said, referring to the woman in the photo.

The inmate nodded. "Yes, she is. And for some crazy reason, she's waiting for me. She doesn't visit so often now, I've told her to focus on her own thing for a while. But she brings me treats every now and then."

"What would you like more of? What are you lacking?" he asked, determined to do something to make it up to him.

"Books," 2666 said, holding up the ragged paperback. "There's really not much choice in here."

"Okay, I'll arrange for you to have some credit to choose some books you'd like to read, as an apology for what happened, and a thank you for helping me."

The inmate's face lit up, but then he frowned. "You don't have to do that."

"I know, but I want to."

The inmate smiled, and Oscar grinned back.

"Will I see you on shift soon?"

Oscar shook his head. "I've had to quit. They can't have epileptic guards working in a prison."

"Oh, that sucks." The inmate stood and offered his hand. Oscar could feel Jason's resistance to the contact, but he ignored it and shook the man's hand firmly.

Without another word, they nodded at each other and

Oscar and Jason left the cell.

"Are you really going to pay for some books for him?" Jason asked.

"Yes," Oscar said. "The man likes to read, and I want to thank him." When they reached the lounge, they too shook hands, then Oscar headed back to Mick's office. He had a man's name to clear.

CHAPTER ELEVEN

"What happens if one of us meets our Flame?"

Xander looked at Kirsty, who was snuggled into his side under his thick coat as they watched the sunset on the beach. "Do you think it's likely?" he asked. "I mean, what are the chances of meeting them?"

Kirsty shrugged. "I've read a lot of stuff online about people who are finding them more frequently right now. But often the relationship doesn't work out for some reason. There are few that manage to stay together."

Xander frowned. "I don't know what would happen if one of us met our Flames. I can't imagine loving anyone more than you right now."

Kirsty beamed up at him, and Xander smiled back. She really was very beautiful when she shone with joy.

"I love you too," Kirsty said. "I can't imagine wanting to leave you for someone else. I just wondered what we would do if it ever happened."

"I guess all we can do is handle the situation when and if it arises."

Kirsty nodded and looked back at the orange disc in the sky that was about to meet the horizon. "Very wise words."

"My family want me to go home for Christmas," Xander said suddenly, making Kirsty look up at him strangely.

"Do you want to go?" she asked.

"No, not at all."

"Problem solved. Let's stay here and do what we planned to – have an awesome Christmas party, then eat too much, listen to cheesy eighties songs, play monopoly then sleep a lot."

Xander grinned. "Sounds like a much better plan to me. I'll tell my mum that I'm too busy."

"Excellent," Kirsty said, snuggling deeper under his jacket and shivering. The sea breeze was particularly wintry, and Xander was grateful for her body heat mingling with his.

"What about your family?" he asked, curious. "Don't they want to see you?"

He felt her body stiffen and wondered if it was an inappropriate question. "I doubt it. We don't really see eye to eye," she said, her vague explanation intriguing him further. He decided to ask the Angels about it later.

The sun disappeared into its watery grave, and after a few moments, Xander slowly stood up, lifting Kirsty up with him.

"Let's go get a hot chocolate before we go home," he said. She nodded and they walked slowly across the pebbly beach back toward town to their favourite café.

When they arrived, they basked in the warmth just inside the front door for a few moments before Kirsty headed to their normal table and he headed to the counter to get the drinks.

"Hi," the barista greeted him, a smile on her face. Xander recognised her as the woman who'd thought he and Kirsty made a good couple.

"Hi," Xander said with a grin. "I guess you were right, after all," he said jerking his head to where Kirsty sat. The woman grinned.

"I'm so glad," she said. "You really do look good together."

"We are good together," Xander agreed, paying for the drinks and the Christmas cookies he chose on a whim.

"See you next time," the woman said.

Xander smiled and put his change in the tip jar before picking up the drinks and cookies then carrying them over to Kirsty, careful not to spill anything. He loved how her face lit up when she saw the cookies. She got so excited about the simplest things, which really lit Xander up too. He felt like his life had been too dark and serious before she had entered it.

"So are you doing readings tomorrow?"

"Yes," Xander said, biting the head off the Santa and chewing it. "I'll probably do more days in the shop in the run up to Christmas, at this time of year, people are beginning to question what they're doing with their lives, and how they can make the next year better, and they come for guidance on what to do."

Kirsty sighed. "I know how they feel."

Xander frowned. What are you needing guidance on?"

"My job," Kirsty said. "It was bad enough that they cut my hours right down, because it means I'm not really earning enough, but now the boss has handed over most of the responsibilities to my manager, which means she's power-drunk and acting like a total idiot. I'm not sure how much longer I can stand to stay there."

"Do you want me to ask your Angel?" Xander asked.

Kirsty smiled. "That sounds like a good idea, I would love to know what it is I'm really meant to be doing. I just feel like I've been floating since I left Uni."

"What subject did you study?" Xander asked, realising then that he knew very little about Kirsty's past. He knew nothing of her family, her upbringing, her education, not even her hobbies or favourite pastimes. Other than kissing him, going to the beach and drinking copious amounts of hot beverages in their favourite café, of course.

"Textiles," Kirsty replied, sipping her caramel-laced hot chocolate and nibbling the body of her snowman.

"But you work in a recruitment agency? Where's the link?"

Kirsty laughed. "That's my point, there isn't one. None of the jobs I've had since I graduated have had anything to do with what I studied. I came here because of the Indie creative scene, but then I just grabbed the first job I could find, so I could pay my rent and bills and still eat."

"I know that feeling," Xander sighed.

"But you enjoy doing the tarot readings?"

"Yes, but for five years I was working in shitty office jobs, just trying to make ends meet. And doing the readings just about pays for my rent and bills, but the only reason I was able to give up my job and do it full time was because of an inheritance I got from my granddad."

Kirsty nodded. "It does feel like it's only possible to do spiritual or creative work if you get outside help. Making a living from it seems a little impossible sometimes."

"That's because we've been conditioned to think that, and because we live in a society that doesn't value creativity as much as it should." He finished the cookies and wiped his mouth with a paper napkin. "So what did you want to do with your degree?"

"I wanted to design my own range of fabrics, for dressmaking. Funky prints that are washable and don't lose their vibrancy."

"That sounds great," Xander said. "Do it."

Kirsty frowned. "How? I don't have the money to get designs copyrighted and fabric made, and I don't have any contacts other than people from Uni."

"Don't worry about the *how*," Xander said, waving his hand. "Focus on the *what* and the *why*. What do you want to do, and why do you want to do it?"

"I want to make funky print fabric, because I think clothing should reflect our personalities, and not just be functional or comfortable. I never found clothing that suited me growing up and I wanted to create designs that would reflect different personalities and moods."

"Awesome, do it. When we get back to my flat get sketching, get designing. Then we will work out the production part when we come to it."

Kirsty shook her head, a half smile on her face. "It's that easy, huh? Just sketch out a few designs and make it happen?"

"Yes, it really is that simple. Life is simple, we're the ones who make it complicated. I'll still have a chat with the Angels though, they might have some ideas for you."

Kirsty nodded. "Thanks. Well, seeing as I've got all my

art stuff at mine, maybe I'll go home tonight, and see what I can come up with. I have some stuff I created in Uni that I'd love to expand."

Though he'd been looking forward to spending a cosy evening in front of the TV with her, he knew that it was important for her to act on this sudden motivation to design fabric.

"Okay," he said. "I'll do a meditation tonight and see what comes up."

"Perfect."

They finished their drinks in silence, and then made their way out of the café into the rapidly falling darkness. Xander pulled his jacket closer around him, and gripped Kirsty's gloved hand tightly as they walked back to her place. He kissed her on the doorstep, then wrenched himself away to make the further fifteen minute journey back to his flat.

When he arrived, his fingers were numb and his cheeks were bright red. It seemed that winter was definitely here.

He slowly took off his layers and turned the heating up a little, then he got himself a glass of water and settled into his chair that he used for readings and meditations.

He said a little invocation, then settled back and closed his eyes. He could feel the presence of his Angels almost instantly.

"Xander, your Flame draws near," his Angel said.

He frowned. "What?" he asked in his mind. "My Twin Flame? She's close by?"

"Yes, she is, and you will come into contact with her soon."

Xander thought about this for a moment. Had the Angels prompted Kirsty's question earlier?

"What about Kirsty's Flame?" he asked. "Is he also near?"

"No, her Flame is not on this Earthly plane, and he is not likely to ever be in her lifetime. It is not in the stars for them to experience this life together."

Without knowing why, Xander felt tears forming and one fell. He knew that meeting her Flame was something that she really wanted, despite her being happy with him at the moment.

"Are you saying I will leave Kirsty?" he asked. "Or that I should?"

"I am not telling you what to do, you know that we do not tamper with free will. I am just letting you know that you will soon be faced with this situation, and you will need to decide whether to give up your relationship with Kirsty and be with your Flame, no matter how difficult the relationship might be, or stay with Kirsty and miss the opportunity for that deep connection that can only be felt in such unions."

Xander sighed deeply. He opened his eyes and sat up, taking his tarot deck from their velvet pouch and shuffling them. Every time he had done a reading for him and his Flame, it had always foretold destruction, pain, suffering and ultimately death. He would see if anything had changed, so he would be able to more easily make a decision when the matter arose.

He cut the deck in three then put it back together, then he picked the top seven cards, doing his favourite spread. As he turned each of them over, then stared at the seven images in turn, he knew that he couldn't have picked a worse combination of cards.

"It's not going to work, is it, between me and my Flame?" he asked his Angel.

"I won't lie," the Angel said. "It will be a dark and difficult road to take."

Xander nodded, staring at the cards. The pain on the faces of the men depicted made his mind up for him.

"I'm going to stay with Kirsty, I want to be with her. We have so much fun together, and we fit together."

"That's because you have a long history together, you are soulmates."

Xander nodded. "Yes. Now," he put the cards back into the deck. "Have you got any advice I can pass on to her about her career?"

As he listened to the Angel's soft words, he steeled his resolve to be strong, and not give into the connection he would feel when he met his Flame. He hoped he had the strength to resist.

CHAPTER TWELVE

Lisa was feeling quite nervous as she pulled into the remaining parking spot outside the Twin Flame Retreat. She had been visiting Violet and Greg regularly, and they had asked her to participate in the next retreat, and help the participants to heal their past traumas that may be stopping them from having a happy Twin Flame relationship.

She had protested at first, because she didn't feel like she had done enough to heal Greg and Violet's issue. Would she really be able to help anyone else?

Lisa got everything she needed out of the boot of the car, and made her way up the path to the house. In a weird way, she felt like she was coming home as she neared the building. She had been spending a lot of time there recently, but she'd never felt this way before.

When the door opened and light spilled out into the dim late afternoon, all thoughts of homecoming flew out of her mind, and she gave her Old Soul friend a sideways hug, while still holding onto her box.

"So good to see you!" Violet said. "The guests are all in

their pods, resting before the evening session, just tell me what you need, and we'll get you set up."

"Sorry I couldn't get here earlier, it was pretty crazy at the shop today, my sessions were booked back to back with no breaks, then I grabbed my stuff and came right over."

"In that case..." Violet took the box from her arms and headed to the kitchen. Lisa followed her, and Violet put the box down on the counter, put the kettle on, and then proceeded to ladle out a bowl of soup and place a slab of homemade bread on a plate. Lisa's stomach growled loudly at the sight of the food, and she didn't even bother to protest. She sat down at the counter and accepted the food with a smile.

"You are seriously an Angel," she said dunking the bread into the soup and then stuffing it into her mouth.

Violet chuckled. "Apparently I was, a very long time ago." She smiled. "I was the Angel of Fate. Starlight, my sister, who is on Earth in human form now, was the Angel of Destiny."

Lisa's eyebrows shot up. She swallowed the mouthful, ignoring the hot soup scalding her throat. "I knew you were influential in Atlantis, but I had no idea of your history. Wow. So what is the fate of the world?"

Violet shook her head. "To know the future is a dangerous thing. It is best to live in the moment."

"Hmm, either it's not a good outcome, or you don't know," Lisa teased, feeling so much less nervous now she'd eaten and relaxed a little.

Violet chuckled. "I'll leave you to ponder that one," she said. She glanced up at the clock on the wall. "I told everyone to come back in for five o'clock, so we can have a two hour session and then eat dinner at seven. Which gives us twenty minutes to get everything ready. Is that cool?"

Lisa nodded and continued to eat. A thought occurred to her then. "Am I eating their dinner?"

"Don't worry, there's plenty of food. The soup is just a starter. You're welcome to eat with us later too. Greg is cooking the main."

Knowing how good a cook he was, Lisa nodded enthusiastically. "I'd love that, thank you." She finished her soup a little too quickly, on account of her hunger and the fact they didn't have long to set up, then she followed Violet upstairs to the workshop room to prepare for the session.

She'd bought some incense that she felt helped people to relax and get into the right state, and she'd also brought a candle that would be placed in the centre of the circle, as a focal point. She found that not everyone enjoyed meditating with their eyes closed, some needed a point of focus in order to quiet their minds and open up.

She set everything up in less than ten minutes, and just before five, she heard the front door opening and the muted voices of the participants.

"I'll go down to get them, are we ready?" Violet asked.

Lisa nodded, the nerves beginning to flutter in her stomach again.

She settled herself on a cushion, and closed her eyes for a few moments to centre herself before she heard footsteps on the stairs as the group came upstairs to join her. She remained where she was, and sensed everyone coming into the room and settling on the cushions in a circle. The feeling of being home suddenly washed over her again, but she ignored it and opened her eyes to smile at the group.

This retreat was specifically for couples who were in Twin Flame relationships, so they were sat in pairs. She took her time to make eye contact with each one before she greeted them and introduced herself.

There was a murmur of greetings in return, and then she launched into a short explanation of what they were about to do.

Essentially, she was going to take them back to a time when in the past when they were with their Flame, and heal anything that happened then, that might be affecting the present.

"Everyone ready?" she asked, looking around them again. They all nodded, and Lisa instructed them to either focus on the candle flame in the centre or to close their eyes and listen to her voice.

She guided them through the maze and mists of time to their previous life, and found herself getting flashes of images. Intrigued by the scenes she witnessed, she asked the images to slow down so she could see them properly, and found herself thrown into a scene that looked like it was in Atlantis. She was walking down the jewelled street, when a couple walked by, embroiled in an argument. Her eyes met the man's and a jolt went through her of recognition, of knowing. Of being home.

Her eyes widened, and as they passed by, she turned to look back, and found that he was doing the same.

Was he her Twin Flame?

She shook herself a little, and then after the participants had had long enough to experience what they needed to, she softly brought them back through the maze to the present. When they opened their eyes, she pointed to the paper and pens, and encouraged them to write down their experiences, so they could discuss how they could heal the issue. She turned on some low lights, so they could see enough to write, and when she sat back down, she locked eyes with one of the guys who wasn't writing anything, but just staring at her.

He was the man in Atlantis. She broke her gaze away to look at his partner. It was the same woman.

She looked back at him to find he was still staring at her. He knew. She could tell.

Her cheeks bright red and heart beating furiously, she excused herself from the circle to use the bathroom, and encouraged them to continue recording their visions.

"Holy shit," she muttered to herself when she got to the bathroom, glad that the whirring fan would drown out her voice.

That sense of being home. That knowing, that feeling of belonging, he was her Flame, she just knew it.

She'd sensed him as soon as she'd pulled up that afternoon. Her soul had known he was here.

But he was here with his partner, who he believed to be his Flame, who he wanted to work things out with.

She didn't even need the loo, but she flushed anyway, and then splashed her face and neck with cold water before entering the cosy room again.

Everyone had stopped writing, and were chatting quietly amongst themselves.

"Apologies for the pause, I hope you were all able to recall what you saw. As there are only four couples, we should have enough time to hear each story, and then to perform the necessary healing for each of you." She turned to the first couple and motioned for them to start.

It took a huge amount of concentration to keep her focus on hearing their words, so she could formulate the healing needed. Especially when she heard the couple talk of their stresses in Atlantis. The whole time they spoke, Lisa found that she couldn't look directly at them, partly in fear that they would recognise her from that time.

The session couldn't end fast enough for Lisa. Being in such a close space to someone, whose name she'd learnt during the session was Joseph, who made her feel alive in a way no one ever had before, was unnerving her. Especially as she had only just recently performed a ritual to release her fear of being in a relationship, and to allow the right person to enter her life.

And here he was.

Finally, she was leading a closing meditation, and then they all stood up and stretched to get their blood flowing again, before heading downstairs to eat. The smell of Greg's cooking was filtering up the stairs, but despite the fact that her stomach was growling again, Lisa tried desperately to come up with a reason why she had to leave. She couldn't spend any more time here with this group, it felt too dangerous.

She went downstairs last, grateful that Joseph was pulled out of the room quickly by his wife. She gathered her stuff, leaving the candle behind as the wax was still molten.

She went downstairs slowly, and instead of entering the front room where everyone was seated waiting for dinner, she went through to the kitchen to where Greg was putting the finishing touches on the meal.

"Hey, Lisa," he greeted her. "How did the session go?"

Lisa set the box down on the floor and nodded. "Good, yeah, uh huh."

Greg looked up at her and frowned. Her response hadn't fooled him.

Violet dashed into the kitchen then, and announced that everyone was ready. Lisa offered to help serve and was incredibly relieved when Violet refused and told her to relax.

When the guests were taken care of, Violet then served Lisa with the main meal. "Are you okay eating in the kitchen? I can make a space in the front room with everyone else."

"No, no, I'm good here. Honestly."

Greg gave her another funny look, and Lisa looked down at her plate, and began nibbling at the food.

By the time Violet and Greg had finished serving the guests their starter, main meal and dessert, had cleared the tables and set up a film in the room upstairs, then finally sat down to eat their own meal, they looked exhausted.

Lisa took her plate to the sink and started to do the washing up.

"Oh, Lisa, you don't have to do that, leave it and sit down with us," Violet said.

Lisa shook her head and filled the washing up bowl. "No, it's cool, I actually really like washing up."

"Weirdo," Greg said jokingly, making Lisa laugh.

She plunged her hands into the hot soapy water and lost herself in the menial task.

When the last dish was clean, Lisa reluctantly re-joined her friends at the counter, and sat down again. Violet went to check on the guests, and Greg leaned in toward Lisa, a concerned look on his face.

"What's wrong? What happened during the session?"

Lisa sighed. She should have known she couldn't get away with not saying anything. She told him what she had seen during the meditation, and how she had felt in Joseph's presence.

"Ah," Greg said. "That's, um, yeah. That could be a problem. Do you really think he recognised you?"

"I know he did. But he's here with his wife, to work out how to have a Twin Flame relationship with her. He didn't come here looking for someone else."

"No," Greg agreed. "He didn't. But perhaps that was what was meant to happen. What are you going to do?"

Lisa shook her head. "Nothing. My parents split up because my dad left her for another woman, and my mum was devastated. A few years later, she got cancer, and she died. And knowing what I do about energy, and how emotions affect our bodies, I know that she died because her heart was broken. I will not do that to another woman. I won't."

Greg nodded. "I admire your determination. So what happens now?"

"I go home, feed my dog and go to sleep. Then tomorrow, I go to work and carry on as normal."

"Normal? Who's normal?" Violet asked, catching the last word of her sentence.

"No one," Lisa said with a forced laugh. "I've got to get going, I have a full schedule of healing appointments tomorrow. Thank you so much for inviting me to lead the session tonight," she wrapped her arms around her friend and hugged her tight. "I'll see you soon." She smiled at Greg and picked up her box, feeling incredibly close to tears, but determined to keep herself together.

"See you soon," Greg said.

Lisa nodded and left the kitchen, making her way through the house to the front door. As she passed the stairs, the pull was so strong to go upstairs that she had to force herself to put one foot in front of the other and keep going

Outside, the owls were calling to one another, and knowing that no one could see her now, she allowed the tears to fall freely.

Once she got into her car, it was at least fifteen minutes before she could see well enough to drive home.

*   *   *

"Can I help you?"

Quentin looked up from the display into Delia's eyes and nodded. "Yes, I need help."

She laughed, but when he didn't laugh with her, or even smile, she stopped.

"I'm sorry," she said. "What can I help you with? Was everything okay with Jenna afterward? She seemed to forgive you pretty quickly."

"That's because she assumed that the jewellery I bought from you was an engagement ring. I heard her tell her friend."

"Ah." Delia winced. "That's awkward."

"Can I take you for a coffee? When do you finish work?"

Delia blinked at the sudden invitation, but Quentin didn't care if he was being too forward, he needed to talk to someone, and he had no one to turn to. None of his friends could cope with anything like this, and it wasn't like he could talk to Jenna.

"Um, sure. I finish at five."

"Great, I'll be back then."

Before she could change her mind, he walked away. He glanced at his watch, he had two hours to kill. Sounded like the perfect excuse to go and watch the action film he wanted to see that Jenna refused to go to.

After an hour and forty minutes of pure action and gratuitous violence, Quentin emerged from the darkened cinema into the chilly wintery wind. He headed to the jewellery shop, he had ten minutes to spare.

He got there and waited outside, trying not to look like he was casing the joint. Five minutes after five, Delia emerged, and saw him lurking to the left of the shop.

"Hey," she said. "Where did you want to go?"

Quentin shrugged. "I don't mind, pick your favourite place."

They walked in silence to a tiny little tea shop, outside of the town centre, down an alley. Quentin hadn't even known it existed.

They placed their orders then sat down. Delia raised her eyebrows at him, giving him his cue to begin talking. But the words were stuck in his throat. Their drinks arrived before he could utter a single coherent sentence.

"Are you still against getting married?" she asked softly, prompting him.

He shrugged. "I don't know. She sounded so excited on the phone, talking about whether I would propose on Christmas Day or New Year's. I had no idea she even wanted to get married, she never seemed bothered before. But it seems you were right."

"I usually am," Delia said wryly, making Quentin laugh, and relieving some of the tension in his head.

He sipped his coffee, wincing at the bitterness. He grabbed a couple of packets of brown sugar and dumped them into the cup.

Delia watched his actions, an amused smile on her face. "May I be honest with you?"

Quentin nodded.

"I think that your relationship with Jenna is like your coffee."

Quentin looked down at his cup and frowned at the black liquid. "Excuse me?"

"You ordered something that you felt would be good for you, that you felt you should, but when you tasted it, it was too bitter to be palatable, so you added a heap of sugar to sweeten it, to make it bearable. When really, it would have been better to order something you really wanted in the beginning. But seeing as you've already bought it, the next best thing would be to dump the bitter coffee, go back to the counter and order a new drink. The problem with that is, you feel like you've invested too much in the coffee to just throw it away."

Quentin blinked at her complicated analogy, which had obviously only just occurred to her in that moment. He wanted to protest, but he knew that she was right.

"So what are you going to do? Are you going to persevere, and drink the sweeter yet still bitter – leaves a bad taste in the mouth after – black coffee, or are you going to throw it out and go and order yourself something much more enjoyable and to your taste?"

"You make it sound so simple," Quentin muttered,

now unwilling to pick the cup up. "But coffee is a little less complicated than a relationship."

"Maybe it is, maybe it isn't. We make things as simple or as complicated as we want."

Quentin sighed, wondering if asking Delia had been the right thing to do. Maybe he should have just gone to the pub instead and got wasted.

Delia sipped her drink slowly. She'd ordered a cinnamon-laced hot chocolate which smelled amazing. Clearly, she had no trouble in picking out exactly what she wanted.

What should he do? If he was on his own, and this was just about coffee, he would just keep drinking it, even though it was turning his stomach slightly. But now he had an audience, and the coffee represented his relationship, he had no idea what he should do. He did feel like he'd invested a lot in his relationship with Jenna, and despite her annoying him a little recently, they'd had some amazing times together, and had created a home together. They picked each other up when they were down, they had a great time in the bedroom, most of the time.

Why would he give that up?

Sometimes it may be a little bitter, but most of the time, it was sweet. And wasn't that as much as he could hope for?

His coffee was getting cold while the thoughts ran wild through his mind, and finally, feeling defeated and thirsty, he looked up at Delia and sighed.

"I know you may judge me for this, but," he picked up the lukewarm cup and took a sip.

Delia smiled. "Don't be silly. I'm in no position to judge. I did the same thing. Over and over again."

"Are you still with him then?" Quentin asked, feeling

gutted at the idea that she might have a boyfriend.

"No, he found someone else." She shrugged. "It was for the best, he's very happy now."

"And you? Are you happy?"

Delia smiled. "Yes, I am. Because I know now that I won't order black coffee again by mistake."

Quentin nodded, and slugged down the rest of his drink. "Thank you for your help. I should get home, Jenna will be wondering where I got to, I didn't even tell her I had the afternoon off work today."

"I really hope that you're happy together," Delia said softly. "And maybe I'll see you soon, when you're ready?"

Quentin frowned, wondering if she was hitting on him, but then he saw her holding her ring finger and he realised that she meant see him again soon at the jewellers, to buy a ring.

He nodded. "Yes, I may well see you soon."

He got up and then leaned down to kiss her on the cheek. The brief contact with her skin jolted through him like a thousand volts. He stood up quickly and walked out of the tea shop without a backward glance.

Outside, he took a deep breath, and fought the urge to go back inside. Only a few minutes later, the skies opened up and dumped what felt like a month's worth of ice-cold rain on his head. But instead of being annoyed, Quentin enjoyed it, and by the time he arrived home, he felt cleansed.

CHAPTER THIRTEEN

"I do hope we're not causing you problems by being here," Pearl said to Sarah over coffee just after dawn.

Sarah yawned and shook her head. "Don't worry, this house was never quiet before you arrived, having seven extra people hasn't actually made much difference. My only concern is that you guys don't seem to get much rest, it can't be that comfortable, sleeping on our living room floor?"

Pearl smiled and sipped her drink. "I have spent my entire existence standing by the gates to the Angelic Realm, to lie down, on anything, is something quite extraordinary."

Sarah chuckled. "I guess it is, when you put it that way." She set her cup down and stretched, yawning again.

"I see you are still a nocturnal being," Pearl commented. "Being on Earth hasn't made you into a morning person."

"Nor has having kids or having to get them to school on time," Sarah said, her face in a grimace. "The only reason I'm up early today is because I had an odd dream, and a strong feeling that you and I needed to speak in private. And privacy is something of a rarity here."

Pearl nodded. "I have been waiting to speak with you since we arrived."

"It's about Gold?" Sarah guessed. "It's been too long since I visited him in my dreams, and meditations, I know. Does he ever check in on me?"

"He tries not to. When you first left, he was devastated. He spent all his time in the Angelic Realm watching your life, having left the Indigo Child in charge of the crossings. But I managed to convince him that he needed to let go, to let you live, and to do his own work to the best of his ability, that it really wouldn't be long until you returned. And he has done so ever since."

Sarah nodded. "I knew he would have difficulty with my absence, but I also knew it was important for me to be here."

"He knows that. He knows you are doing what you feel is necessary for the good of humanity."

"So do you have a message for me from him? Did you see him before you left?" Sarah sipped her coffee and rubbed her eyes.

"Yes," Pearl said softly. "He was upset to hear that I would be leaving too, though I said my absence would be even shorter than yours. I asked him if he had a message for you, something he wanted to pass along, and there were two things."

Pearl reached into her pocket and pulled out a wooden pendant on a worn leather string. She handed it to Sarah, who looked at in wonder. "Violet and Greg have necklaces like this," she said, turning it in her hands.

Pearl nodded. "This was Laguz's original necklace. He gave it to Velvet, and then when they left for Earth, it was left in the Atlantis Garden, where Gold then took possession of it. He said it made him feel closer to you, so he wore it, until the day he let go and resumed his work. He asked that I bring it to you. In all honesty, I wasn't even sure it was possible to bring a material item from the Fifth Dimension. But it remained in my hand when I crossed through the mists to this world."

Sarah smiled, reached up to put the necklace on, then touched it gently where it nestled in the hollow of her neck. "What was the second thing?"

Pearl sighed and shook her head. "For the record, I resisted the passing on of this message, I said that it wouldn't be a good idea, but he was insistent."

Sarah frowned. "Please tell me, Pearl. I can handle it."

Pearl remained silent, trying to figure out how to impart the message from her oldest and dearest friend. "He asked me to tell you-"

"Morning!"

Pearl and Sarah jumped. Neither of them had heard Peridot approaching the kitchen. The Angel came in and went straight to the kettle, quite used to the human appliances by now. "What are we doing today?" She looked at the two women standing by the window, in suspended animation, and suddenly realised that she had interrupted something. "Oh, um, sorry, I'll just, I'll come back for a drink, um, in a bit." She retreated from the kitchen, and disappeared out of the door just as the kettle boiled.

"Are you meant to tell me this?" Sarah asked, taking the interruption as a possible sign from the Universe.

"Gold seemed certain you needed to know," Pearl said. "He wanted me to tell you-"

"Muuuuuum! Star won't let me use the bathroom!"

Sarah looked up to see her youngest fly into the kitchen, and she caught him and picked him up, heaving him up onto her hip.

She looked at Pearl and smiled. "Maybe it's not time yet."

Pearl smiled back. "Maybe not." She finished her drink and rinsed out the cup, then went back to where her team of Angels waited for her instruction in the living room.

She sat down on the sofa, and waited for them to stop chattering and go quiet.

"I think you're going to enjoy this task, Angels," she said with a smile. "It's going to save a lot of lives."

*　　*　　*

"Have you eaten anything? Or been outside? Or even noticed that it's a beautiful day today?"

Oscar glanced up at his wife from the computer screen, shook his head then went back to his research. He heard her sigh and leave the room.

He knew he was acting like a crazy man, but for the first time in a long time, he actually felt passionate about something, and he was determined to do something about it.

Before leaving the prison, he had made an official statement to clear the name of inmate 2666, and had also put in a request for his case to be looked at, to see if early parole would be a possibility. The man had served seven years of a ten year sentence, and had never been reported before the incident with his collapse.

He hoped that Mick would take up the case, but in the meantime, he was researching how to get more reading materials into prisons, material that would actually help the inmates to find a better path, not just old crime thrillers. So far, he'd only found one non-profit charity in America that did something like it, called *Freedom Inside*. He had emailed the lady who ran it, and asked her how he could implement something like that in the UK. She created a newsletter that she sent out to prisoners, and they could request books from it, that had been donated. They also wrote poetry and stories that she featured in the newsletters.

When he could ignore his growling stomach no longer, he put his laptop into hibernation and joined his wife in the kitchen where she was making dinner. She had been less than impressed when he'd decided not to take the desk job at the prison, as they now had to exist on her salary and his redundancy pay until he worked out what he was doing next.

"The doctor said it was important for you to eat at regular intervals," she said as soon as he entered the kitchen. "I left out snacks for you, why couldn't you stop for five minutes to eat something?"

Oscar leaned in to kiss her on the cheek. "I know, I'm sorry, I just feel really fired up about this, besides, I haven't had a fit for two days now, so I'm sure it's fine."

"That's not the point. You need to start looking after your body, otherwise you're going to wear it out, and what will I do then?"

Oscar sighed. He loved Emily with everything he had, but sometimes, she just reminded him too much of his mother.

"I promise to eat more regularly tomorrow, okay?"

Emily sighed this time. "Fine. Why don't you get James? Dinner is nearly ready."

Oscar nodded and went upstairs to get his son. Halfway up the stairs, he felt a tremor go through his body, but before he could get to the top to safety, his hand slipped from the bannister and everything went black.

"Greetings, Onyx."

Oscar blinked and looked around, blinded by the white mist swirling around him. He focussed on the man in golden robes before him and he frowned. "Onyx?" he repeated. He blinked then, as his previous existence as an Angel of Protection rushed back to him, making him gasp. "Gold? Holy shit, I'm dead!"

"Indeed. Well, you are in between worlds, currently. You have fallen down the stairs and injured yourself after having an epileptic fit. Your wife is currently trying to revive you, and has called for an ambulance."

Oscar blinked at the information and shook his head. "Right, wow, um, what should I do?"

"Do you want to stay? Or do you want to return to Earth?"

Oscar thought for a moment. "I do feel like I'm finally passionate about things, for the first time in a long while. Haven't felt like this since I was in the army."

Gold waited patiently for him to continue.

"But I also know that my life isn't what I imagined it would be. When I left here, it was with the feeling and hope in my heart that I would be reunited with my Twin Flame and that we would get to have a human life together." As his Flame came into his consciousness, it felt like an arrow to his heart. He had been asleep in his human life to the wonder and joy he had felt in his Flame's presence. "I love my wife, but I wonder if it's a good idea, being with her when I feel like there's someone out there who I'm waiting for."

"Waiting for? You have already crossed paths with your Flame," Gold said. "You just may not have recognised her at the time."

Oscar frowned. "I've already met her? Are you sure?"

"Positive," Gold said.

Oscar thought of his Flame's face, her energy, then ran his life through his mind and tried to match the energies together. When he hit on a match, he gasped again.

"Louise!" He thought of his girlfriend in school, and how awful it had been to leave her when he joined the army. But he had been determined back then, to make a difference, to change the world. Instead, he had just been part of a mission of mass-destruction and death. Tears began to fall and his heart ached. She hadn't been willing to wait, she hadn't wanted to be worried about him all the time, wondering if he was okay. She had told him to choose, and he had chosen war.

He hung his head. She was his Flame? It made sense. The way they had fit together, the way they could tell each other everything. He had even had dreams of her while in the war. Dreams so vivid, that he would wake up having forgotten where he was.

"Yes, Louise," Gold said, his voice gentle. "She understands the choice that you made. That your need for following your mission was stronger than your need for her love."

"I don't understand though, why did I not see her, see the relationship for what it was?"

"It wasn't the right time," Gold said. He tilted his head. "Actually, that's not strictly true. It wasn't the right time for you. She was ready."

Oscar felt even worse. He hadn't had any communication with her since that day. Even though he had been desperate to write to her. But the years passed, he met his wife, then she left the army to have their son, then he'd been injured in action, and they had been in a comfortable routine ever since.

"It's time to decide. Your body is now in the ambulance, they have stabilised you, you have a fairly severe head injury."

"Will I be permanently disabled?" Oscar asked. The idea of being trapped in a useless body made him want to stay on the Other Side.

"No, in fact, it may improve things."

Oscar laughed. He hadn't realised that Gold had a sense of humour.

"Will I get to be with my Flame if I go back?" he asked.

The Elder remained silent. "I'm afraid I cannot predict that."

Oscar sighed. He figured the old man wouldn't give him all the answers. He thought of Louise again and smiled. Even if he went back, and just met up with her again to see if she was okay, and to apologise for being an idiot, it would be worth it.

"I want to go back," he said, making the decision.

Gold nodded. "Very well." He held his hand out to the Angel, who shook it. "I wish you the best, Onyx."

"Thank you." Oscar turned away from the Elder and walked into the mist, until it got too bright to keep his eyes open.

When he opened them again, and returned to his body, the pain of his injuries hit him full force, and he wondered if he'd made a terrible mistake.

CHAPTER FOURTEEN

"Merry Christmas!"

Xander engulfed Kirsty in a hug and kissed her. She melted into his embrace, and he breathed in her scent of oranges and cinnamon.

She pulled back and grinned up at him. "Merry Christmas to you too," she said.

He ushered her inside and took her coat, and she shivered as she acclimatised to the temperature inside. She looked around, amazed by how beautifully he'd decorated his flat. "When is everyone else coming?"

"Around seven, nearly ready now, just need to get the mulled wine on and the mince pies out of the oven."

"Nice," Kirsty said. "Shall I get some music on? You got your tablet? I'll find a Christmas channel on YouTube."

Xander handed Kirsty his tablet, then went to the kitchenette to get the pies out of the oven. He was really looking forward to the evening, and had a fluttering feeling of excitement in his stomach. He poured the bottle of wine into the saucepan and smiled. The fluttering feeling could of course be due to the fact that he'd already drunk half a bottle of wine to himself though. He found that having a few drinks made him less receptive to the spirit world, which was ironic, when you thought about it. Made it easier to be around a lot of people when you couldn't also see their Guardian Angels.

He heard traditional Christmas carols and then felt Kirsty's arms encircle his waist from behind.

"Smells amazing," she said. "Did you make the pies yourself?"

"Um, well, no, afraid not," Xander said with a sheepish smile. "I may have had a little help from Kipling. I just warmed them up."

Kirsty giggled and gave him a squeeze. "That's cool, I think it would be a bit weird if you really were that domesticated."

Xander stopped stirring the wine and turned to face her. He put his hands around her waist and lifted her up, making her squeal. She wrapped her legs around his waist and he kissed her deeply. "Nothing domesticated about me," he said with a growl, when they came up for air.

Kirsty giggled and kissed him again. "Feel free to let your inner animal out any time you like," she purred.

The doorbell rang then, and Kirsty sighed as he set her down on her feet. "Time to be social," he said. He bent down to whisper in her ear. "Later."

She shivered with delight and he went to answer the door. He welcomed his friends and neighbours in, and soon the flat was fit to burst. The mince pies were a hit, and he was pouring the fourth bottle of wine into the saucepan to heat up when the hair on the back of his neck stood up and he felt the presence of someone behind him. He shrugged it off, assuming it was just a spirit who'd made it through the drunken haze, and was startled when he heard a soft voice behind him.

"Great party."

He turned around, but even as he did, he knew that it would be a mistake. He blinked at the woman stood before him, and the glow of her aura around her body was so bright he almost felt like he could touch it. He frowned. He knew he didn't recognise her, but at the same time, he felt as though he'd known her all his life.

"Astrid," she said, holding out her hand. "I came with Walter, hope that's okay."

He nodded slowly, wishing he hadn't had so much to drink. "Uh, yeah, that's cool, the more the merrier and all."

She nodded, and lowered her unshaken hand, but she had a strange expression on her face, like she was trying to figure out who he was. "Have we met before?" she asked finally, after several moments of awkward silence punctuated by laughter coming from the living room.

Xander shook his head quickly, then regretted it as the room started to spin.

"Um, are you okay? You look like you're about to throw up?" she asked.

He shook his head again, then knew that he was going to have to run if he was to make it to the bathroom in time.

Luckily, it wasn't engaged, and he was even able to lift the toilet seat before he lost the contents of his stomach. He felt a little like Stan off South Park.

"Here."

To his utter horror and embarrassment, he flushed the

toilet and turned around to see Astrid holding out a glass of water out to him. He closed the toilet lid and sat on it, then slugged down the water, hoping to calm his stomach.

"Guess you had a little too much mulled wine, eh?" she joked.

He nodded, feeling incapable of speech.

"What's going on, are we partying in the bathroom?"

Xander heard Kirsty's voice and didn't know whether to feel relieved or horrified.

"Xander's had a little too much wine and has been ill," Astrid said politely, stepping out of the room to allow Kirsty to come into the tiny space.

Xander tried to reassure his girlfriend that he was fine and had just had a little too much, all the while wondering if he would ever see his Twin Flame again.

*   *   *

"Thank you so much for inviting me over, I really appreciate it."

Violet smiled at Lisa as Charlotte and Daniel, Julie's children, fought each other with plastic swords in front of them.

"It was our pleasure, couldn't have you sitting home alone, even though Missy is a wonderful companion." Violet stroked Lisa's dog behind the ears, where she slept contentedly on her lap.

Lisa laughed. "Yeah, I should have taught her how to pull a cracker though, difficult to do that by yourself."

"More mulled wine, guys?"

Violet and Lisa both nodded to Julie, who was helping

Greg in the kitchen.

They heard the bell ringing by the front door and Missy leapt from Violet's lap, and barked.

"Oh good," Violet said. "That will be the others."

Lisa hadn't realised more people were coming, and when she felt a wave of familiarity wash over her, she had a sinking feeling of who would be coming through the door.

When the first two people came through the door, she felt a mixture of relief and disappointment, as she didn't recognise them.

"Tim! Hannah!" Julie said, coming through the living room to greet the couple. She gave them both a hug and introductions were made, but when Violet returned to the lounge, she had two more people in tow. Sure enough, it was the couple from the retreat.

Lisa's eyes met Joseph's, and a jolt of electricity shot through her.

"Lisa, you remember Joseph and Joanna? From the retreat?"

Lisa nodded mutely, and tried to smile, but her face had seized up. Greg came into the room, which suddenly felt incredibly claustrophobic with eight adults and three children in it.

"Lisa, could you give me a hand a minute?" Greg asked.

Lisa nodded and followed him out of to the kitchen, where he touched her arm and lowered his voice so the others wouldn't hear.

"Are you okay? I'm so sorry there was no warning, Violet just said she'd invited a couple from the retreat, I had no idea who it was."

Lisa felt her eyes fill and she shook her head. "It's okay," she whispered.

"It's obviously not," Greg said, concern in his eyes. "What do you want to do, do you want to stay? I can take you home if not, though I'd hate for you to be at home on your own."

Lisa shook her head again and wiped her eyes with her sleeve. "No, it's okay, really." She squared her shoulders. "I can be in the same room as him. I'll just stay out here with you until dinnertime if that's okay. And then I might just go to bed early."

Greg nodded, concern still written all over his face. "Okay, just let me know what I can do to make it easier."

Lisa nodded. "Thank you."

She could hear the muted conversation in the other room, but couldn't hear any individual words. Julie came back out to the kitchen to help, and as the three of them prepared the meal for everyone, they laughed and joked around and Lisa felt her energy lighten up a little. By the time they lay all the food out on the tables out in the front room, with the children in the dining room, Lisa felt much better. Greg had laid her place as far away from Joseph's as possible, and she was very glad to have his help in coping with the situation.

She could feel Joseph's gaze on her for most of the meal, and Missy, her traitorous little dog, had taken a complete shine to him and was nestled at his feet the whole time.

She listened to the others chatting, and heard Tim and Hannah's amazing story of how they met at the retreat, the accident, Hannah's death and then their reunion. She tried to close down the glimmer of hope that had begun to rise up, that she and Joseph could be united, and have a chance together.

She glanced over to where he sat and her gaze met his. His expression was one of wonder, curiosity and love, and she knew then that he felt the connection between them as strongly as she did. She took a deep breath, broke eye contact and started talking to Julie about how she could start promoting her healing practice in the New Year.

In the previous couple of weeks, she had been seeking out premises to use as her own private healing practice, and she'd found a few that were suitable, she just needed to take the leap now and make it happen.

The conversation took her mind off of Joseph enough for her to enjoy her meal, though it seemed to be sitting heavily in her stomach. She jumped at the chance to help Greg clean the kitchen afterwards, but Violet insisted that they leave all the dishes, and that they all retire upstairs for a Christmas film in the workshop room.

The idea of being in an enclosed, dark space with Joseph made Lisa's heart race, and she wasn't sure she would be able to do it. She dawdled as long as she could downstairs, and before she could gather up the courage to join the others, she heard footsteps coming down the stairs, and knew it was him.

He stepped into the living room where she stood in the centre, frozen, and when their eyes met, Lisa stopped breathing for a few moments.

"We need to talk," he said, his voice low. She shook her head. "I don't think that's a good idea," she whispered. "Please just go back upstairs to your wife."

"I can't," Joseph said, stepping closer. "Ever since the retreat I haven't been able to get you out of my mind. You were there, in Atlantis, I saw you."

Lisa bowed her head. It seemed there was no way of getting out of the situation. "Yes, I was there."

"My wife is not my Twin Flame," he said.

Lisa took a deep breath and looked up at him, to find he was standing just a few inches away. "No," she said softly.

"But you are," he said, his eyes searching hers.

Unable to speak, she nodded, and before she could do anything to stop him, he reached out to touch her cheek. Then he leaned forward and when his lips met hers, it was all she could do not to burst into tears.

The feelings of peace, safety, passion, desire, joy and unconditional love enveloped her in their embrace and Lisa wanted to stay in that place forever. But she reluctantly came to her senses and pulled back and opened her eyes.

"We can't," she said. "You're married, and I won't break up your relationship."

Joseph looked at her like she'd just stabbed him in the heart. "I need you," he whispered urgently. "That was the most amazing kiss I have ever experienced. Didn't you feel it?"

Lisa had to make a decision. If she admitted her feelings for him, told him that she could feel the depth of their connection, there would be no going back, there would be no way out. She had to lie. She had to force him to return to his gorgeous wife and their life together.

"No," she said. I didn't."

He frowned, not believing her lie for a second, but not knowing how to respond.

"Everything okay?"

Lisa jumped out of her skin at the sound of Greg's voice

from the doorway. She thanked the Angels it was him who had come to find them, and not Violet or worse, Joanna.

"Yes, I was just telling Joseph about my new healing practice," Lisa lied smoothly, knowing that she would probably end up telling Greg the truth later anyway. She looked at him and could see he already knew the truth.

"Cool, well we're about to start the film, just thought you might not want to miss the beginning."

"We'll be right up," Lisa said.

Greg nodded and left the room, and she heard his footsteps on the wooden stairs.

Lisa looked at Joseph, who had remained mute and motionless throughout the exchange. "We can't do this," she said softly. "There's too much at stake for you, too much for you to lose. And I won't be the one who makes you lose it all."

"What if it's what I choose to do? What if I decide to leave my wife so I can ask you out?"

"Why would you do that? Please think of her in this, think of your life together, of the commitment you made to each other. From what I've seen of Twin Flame relationships, they're not picnics at the park, they're crazy rollercoasters where emotions are heightened, where limits are pushed and buttons are pressed. It's challenging and painful and heart-breaking and-"

"Deep, wonderful, joyful, incredible, loving, and beautiful," Joseph finished, cutting her off mid-rant. "And I want to experience it all, the good and the bad." He touched her cheek again. "With you."

In that split second, she nearly caved, but the anguished expression on her mother's face when their father left them flashed through her mind and she shook her head vehemently. "No. Don't leave your wife. Don't give up the life you have created. I don't want to be with you."

Lisa refused to look at his face as she left the living room and went upstairs to join the others. She knew that if she saw any kind of pain or anguish on his face she would relent, and she needed to stick to her guns.

She let herself be absorbed by the film, which was a cheesy Christmas one, chosen by Violet. She was aware of Joseph returning to the room, and that he was sat next to his wife, with the traitorous Missy curled up in his lap, but she refused to look his way or acknowledge him.

She was pleased when the film had a sad scene in it, because she then used that as an excuse to allow the bottled tears to fall. Her heart ached and she relived the moment of their lips touching in her mind. Could she really live the rest of her life without ever experiencing that again?

It seemed she would have to find out.

CHAPTER FIFTEEN

True to his word, Quentin had done everything in his power to make their Christmas amazing, and despite the fact that the needles from the tree drove him crazy, especially when they got into his socks, he had to admit he was enjoying it all.

He had bought Jenna an engagement ring, but he had gone to a jewellers in a neighbouring town. He hadn't wanted to see Delia again, it just felt too dangerous to do that, considering she had such a strong effect on him.

He hadn't proposed yet, even though it was getting late in the day, and he could see Jenna was getting more and more jittery as the day wore on.

The ring was safely ensconced inside a bauble he'd put on the tree already, and he was just gathering up the courage to direct her to it, and pop the big question.

He poured himself a glass of mulled apple cider, and took a slug of it, needing the alcohol to calm his nerves. His stomach was churning and his breathing was shallow. He hoped that it was all sign of excitement, not dread; he had trouble differentiating the two sometimes.

He re-joined Jenna in the lounge, where she was wearing her new watch, slippers and even the jumper he'd got her. She smiled up at him, and he handed her a glass of cider.

"You okay?" he asked as he settled on the sofa next to her.

"Yes," she said. "Thank you for all my beautiful gifts, you really did go a bit overboard, but I love it."

Quentin frowned at her as though something just occurred to him. "Hmm, hang on, I think there might be just one more."

Jenna's eyes widened and he motioned to the tree.

"Check out the snowman bauble."

She set her glass down on the coffee table, then went over to the tree, looking like she hardly dared to get excited, just in case it wasn't what she thought. When he heard the click of the bauble catch opening and her gasp, he smiled. She turned to face him, tears running down her cheeks.

He got up and joined her by the tree. Figuring he should do the whole bit, he got down on one knee, wincing slightly as the pine needles pierced his trousers, and he took Jenna's hand in his.

"Jenna, I know I haven't been the easiest person to live with, and I don't always appreciate what an amazing woman you are, but if you'll have me, I would like to make that up to you, and I would like to spend my life with you, building a home, and a life together that we both love."

Her tears were streaming faster and Quentin was worried that his words hadn't been romantic enough.

Finally, after what felt like an eternity, she nodded and he sighed in relief. He took the bauble from her, lifted the ring out then put it on her finger. Then he stood up and she threw her arms around him, and he kissed her. He breathed in her scent, but in the moment that he committed himself to the woman he loved, he couldn't help but think of Delia.

*　　*　　*

"You're a beautiful Angel."

Pearl smiled at the small child with no hair and tubes attached to every part of her small body, and fought the tears that threatened to spill over.

"You should see my real wings," she whispered to the child, who grinned with delight.

Their Christmas mission had been to dress as Angels and visit a children's hospital, to bring love and good cheer to the souls who were ill and suffering. The team were thrilled to be doing something more light-hearted after the few tough missions they'd had. Despite the lives they'd saved, many had still been lost, and they were starting to feel heavy and disheartened.

What Pearl hadn't told them, was that they weren't just there to make the children happy. They were there to heal them.

She reached out to the child, who mirrored her actions. When their hands touched, Pearl sent her the love and light of all the heavens, and the child breathed in deeply suddenly and let out a contented sigh.

She smiled at the child. "All will be well now, do you understand me? Ask to leave this place, you will be just fine."

The child nodded, colour already coming to her cheeks,

her eyes sparkling just a little brighter. Her parents arrived then, and Pearl chatted to them for a few moments. They loved the idea of the Angels coming to visit and granting wishes.

By the time Pearl left the bedside, the child looked completely different. Pearl knew that she would be just fine.

"Pearl?"

Pearl looked up to see Peridot approaching her, and the sight of the Angel with fake white feathered wings on her back made her smile.

"Yes?"

The Angel got close enough to whisper to her.

"We are here to heal, yes?"

Pearl nodded. She knew that her team would get the idea once they started meeting the children. After all, many of them were Crystals and Indigos, and the world needed them in order to move into the Golden Age.

Peridot sighed. "There is one child I fear we are too late for. I can already see her Guardian Angel ready to take her home."

Pearl nodded. "Where?"

Peridot led her to another room, and Pearl peered through the circular window to see a tiny child, enshrouded in white sheets, her bed surrounded by her family.

The idea of losing a child on Christmas Day filled Pearl with horror. "Do you think they would mind?" she asked Peridot.

The Angel shrugged. "I don't know if they will welcome the intrusion."

Pearl looked back through the window and saw the child's Guardian Angel smile at her. She waved for Pearl to enter, so Pearl took a deep breath and pushed open the door. No one turned to look at her, no one noticed her entrance. They were all too focussed on the child whose spirit was slipping away.

"It's her time, Pearl, she's ready."

Pearl nodded to the Guardian Angel, and sent a thought back to her.

"But will the grief of losing her help this family to complete their missions, or will it derail them?"

The Guardian Angel looked back to the bed where the child lay. "Any healing or recovery now would be seen as miraculous, and the child would be seen as a symbol that when all seems to be lost, it's possible for the light to shine through, for love to bring people back from the very edge."

Pearl smiled. "That doesn't answer my question, yet is does at the same time."

She moved to the foot of the bed, and still, no one took any notice of her, except for a small boy on the lap of one of the adults. His grey eyes were wide and he watched Pearl touch the foot of the dying child through her blankets.

She closed her eyes and asked all of the Angels of the Angelic Realm to send their energy through her to the child, to heal her ravaged body, for the damage to be reversed until only light and love filled her to the brim.

She felt the Guardian Angel lay her hand on her shoulder, adding her energy to the huge surge that went through Pearl's body, and flowed through her fingertips to the child. After a few minutes, Pearl opened her eyes and watched as the child's breathing stabilised, as colour returned to her skin, and as she transformed before her very eyes to the point where she opened her eyes, making the woman next to her gasp.

"Kasey?" she whispered, her voice choked with emotion.

"Mum, I'm thirsty," the girl said.

Pearl smiled as her mum started laughing, then sobbing, and the man next to her wrapped his arms around her and together they sobbed in relief.

Pearl smiled at the little boy watching her, then smiled at the Guardian Angel and left the room before anyone else noticed her presence.

Outside the room, she nodded at Peridot, who had been watching through the tiny window. "She's going to make it," Pearl whispered. She blinked, feeling a little faint.

"You need to ground yourself. That was a lot of energy you just channelled, I could see it from here." Peridot took her arm and led her to some chairs to sit down.

Pearl breathed in deeply and sent any excess energy into the floor through her feet, and her head began to feel a little clearer.

"That little boy will always think that the Christmas miracle of his sister coming back to life was because of an Angel," Peridot said with a smile.

"I hope so," Pearl said. "This world needs more belief in us, in the Angelic Realm. Because then perhaps they would listen to our whispers."

CHAPTER SIXTEEN

"Oscar, there's someone at the door."

Oscar left his son playing with his new toys in the lounge, and went to the door where Emily stood, looking uncertain about allowing the visitor into the house.

Oscar's eyes widened when he saw who it was.

"I'm sorry to bother you today, of all days, but I just had to thank you." The man held out a hamper of food to them, and Oscar took it from him, feeling amazed, and slightly unnerved at how he knew where he lived.

"Please," he said, "Come on in."

"I wasn't planning to stay, my wife is in the car; we didn't want to bother you."

"No, I insist," Oscar said, ignoring looks from Emily. "Please go get her and come in for a drink."

The man nodded and then returned moments later with his wife.

They settled into the lounge with drinks, and Emily broke the silence.

"So, who are you?" she asked bluntly, making Oscar

wince.

The man smiled. "My name is Charlie, and this is Ceri, my wife. Your husband did me an extremely big favour a little while back, and it has changed my life. I managed to find his address, and I wanted to come and thank him personally."

Oscar was pleased that Charlie hadn't mentioned he was a previous inmate of the prison where he'd worked; that would have freaked Emily out completely.

"Oh," Emily said, looking at Oscar quizzically, no doubt wondering what the favour was. He knew he'd have to concoct a story later to satisfy her.

"It was my pleasure, Charlie," he said. "I'm happy that things have improved so quickly. And I'm pleased to finally meet your lovely wife."

Ceri beamed at him, her hand firmly in Charlie's. "Yes, thank you for your help. It has really made this Christmas for us."

Oscar nodded, appreciating her vagueness. He could fob Emily off with something army-related.

"What's your plan for the new year?" he asked.

"I'm getting a new job," Charlie said. "And we're going to save up to travel. Have the honeymoon that we didn't have the chance to have."

Oscar nodded. He'd seen in his notes that they'd married in the prison.

They drank their mulled wine in silence for a bit, the only sound was the fake fire crackling on the wall and James playing with his new toys.

After a while, Charlie made movements to leave. But before getting up, he motioned to Ceri and she pulled out a rectangular gift-wrapped package from her bag. Charlie took it from her and held it out to Oscar.

"I thought you might enjoy this," Charlie said. "It brought me a lot of comfort."

Oscar nodded and took the package.

"Open it when we've left," Ceri said with a smile. She rose to her feet and Charlie followed suit. Oscar couldn't help but notice that they were perfectly in sync with each other, and seemed to glow in each other's presence. It tugged at something deep in the crevices of his memory, but he couldn't think what it was.

"Thank you so much for coming to visit us," he said, setting the package down and holding his arms out to embrace the man. They hugged for a few moments, and then he shook Ceri's hand.

The two of them said their goodbyes, then left, and Oscar had the feeling he wouldn't be seeing them again. He knew they were going to go and make the most of their new life together.

"Who the hell were they?" Emily demanded the moment the door closed. Oscar sighed.

"Just an old army buddy that I hooked up with some contacts," he said, the lies rolling off his tongue easily. "It must have panned out, so they came to thank me."

"With a massive food hamper and another gift?" Emily looked at the brightly wrapped basket dubiously, but she was beginning to thaw, he could tell. He wrapped his arms around her. "It meant a lot to Charlie, he'd been needing a break for a few years now. I just put in a good word for him."

Emily nodded and relaxed into his arms. "He had a

sadness in his eyes, something I can't quite explain."

"He's been through some shit," Oscar said. He felt her tense a little, and he guessed she was remembering the time he was shot.

"Hey," he said, turning her around. "I love you. And I'm sorry that it's been a bit tough recently, but I think this New Year is going to be amazing."

Emily smiled and nodded. "At least you haven't had any fits since your last accident," she said.

Oscar frowned. That was true. He'd been so busy trying to make Christmas amazing for his son that he hadn't noticed. Something glimmered in the back of his mind, a distant memory, but it was too nebulous to grasp.

"Are you going to open your gift?" James asked, coming out to the hallway, holding the rectangular package.

Oscar released Emily and took the gift, then they returned to the lounge where he opened it. It was a book that Oscar had never heard of. He read the title silently and wondered why Charlie thought he would like it. With a shrug, he settled into the sofa and began to read.

*   *   *

"Do you want to go to the seafront for New Year's to watch the fireworks?" Kirsty asked Xander as they watched TV on Boxing Day.

Xander nodded absently. He knew that he hadn't been fully with it since the Christmas party, and felt bad for being a bit distant over the Christmas period.

"When you're ready to tell me what's up, I'm ready to listen," Kirsty said, picking up on his thoughts with spooky accuracy.

He sighed. "I'm sorry, I know I've not been with it recently."

"You've been weird since the party. I chalked it up to being ill from drinking too much, but it was four days ago, so what is it?"

Xander sat up straighter, and Kirsty did the same, and reached over to grab the remote and switch the TV off.

His mind was racing. If he told her the truth, there was no way that she would stand in the way of him pursuing his Twin Flame. And if he insisted on staying with her, then she would always feel second best, or that she was holding him back. Then there was the matter of her Flame not being on this planet...

He focused on her in the present moment, and found she was watching him curiously and waiting patiently for him to formulate the words to speak.

"There was someone at the party I wasn't expecting to see," he said, still unsure whether he should tell her the whole truth.

"Astrid," Kirsty said matter of factly. Xander should have known her female intuition would have picked up on the tension.

He nodded. "Yes. Astrid."

"Your Twin Flame?" Kirsty asked bluntly.

Xander's eyes widened. She could make a living as a psychic if she wanted, easily. He nodded again. "Yes, I think so. I mean, we barely spoke, and then I threw up, and then she left, but there was something about her I can't explain."

Kirsty sighed and looked down. Xander could see the conflict in her face. After a few moments, she looked up again.

"You should call her," she said softly. "If she is your Flame, you should be with her."

Xander smiled at her pure selflessness. He wondered if he would have been able to do the same if their positions had been reversed. He shook his head. "No, it's best if I leave it. I don't want to get her hopes up only to disappoint her."

Kirsty frowned. "Why would you disappoint her?"

"Because I wouldn't leave you for her," Xander said, reaching out to tuck a stray hair behind her ear.

"What? Are you crazy? We're not talking about some random woman here, if we were, I'd be upset. This is your Twin Flame, your true ultimate soulmate, why the hell would you not jump at the chance to be with her?"

"Because what we have is too damned good to ruin," Xander replied. "I wasn't going to tell you, but I knew you'd pick up on the craziness in my head, and I can't lie to you. But please know that I am telling you the truth when I say I would rather stay with you than be with Astrid."

"I still don't understand," Kirsty said. "Why? How can you resist the temptation to be with her? It makes no sense. I don't know if I could do the same thing if I had met my Flame."

Xander sighed. "It's not easy," he admitted. "My head and heart have been at war for the past few days. But the truth is, I know that it would be a difficult journey for us, and that the pain and suffering may actually outweigh the good stuff. But with you, I get to be happy and enjoy your beauty and support you in your dreams, and I can see that our road ahead would be easy, and safe."

Xander could feel Kirsty retreating further away from him, and he wondered what part of what he'd said was causing her to react. After several moments of silence, he couldn't bear it any longer. "What is it?"

Kirsty looked into his eyes. "Why would you choose a safe and boring, known path, when you have the choice to go for the unknown, exciting, possibly dangerous but mostly amazing path?"

When put like that, it made him sound like a complete wuss. Should he tell her the full truth? That her Flame wasn't here? And that he couldn't bear to think of her on her own? He didn't want to think that he was sacrificing his own happiness out of pity for her though. So how to word it?

"I think I need to go home," Kirsty said, getting up from the sofa.

Xander frowned. "Don't go. It's freezing out there now. Please stay. I'm sorry, I never intended to make you feel bad." He stood up and wrapped his arms around her. "I guess I choose to stay with you because I'm in love with you. And I've never felt so happy in a relationship before, and I'm too selfish to give that up."

She relaxed into his arms and he hoped that meant that he had finally said the right thing.

"I love you too, but it seems so selfish of me to not give you the chance to be with your Flame."

Xander pulled back a little, then leaned down to kiss her. She didn't respond at first, but soon she was kissing him back, with a passion and fervour that made ripples of excitement run through his body. She didn't resist when he led her to the bedroom, switching off the lights behind him.

CHAPTER SEVENTEEN

"Happy New Year, Missy," Lisa said to her dog as she watched Big Ben chime in London on the TV. Her dog barely lifted her head to look at her; she'd been in a bad mood with her since Christmas. It was ridiculous to think that Missy might be missing Joseph as much as she was, but then anything was possible.

She had been invited to Violet and Greg's place again, but had declined in case she'd found herself in another awkward situation. But part of her wished she'd gone there now. Drinking most of a bottle of wine by herself had made her feel quite depressed.

She switched off the TV as the crowds began to sing Auld Lang Syne, and hauled herself out of the chair, deciding it would be better to just get a glass of water and go to bed. She knew she should set some New Year's resolutions, but then she never stuck to them anyway, so what was the point?

She stood still for a moment to allow her head to stop spinning, and frowned. What was the point of any of it?

Here she was on Earth, knowing that she wouldn't be

with her Flame, knowing that any difference she could possibly make was minimal without him. Yet she had no intention of breaking up his marriage. Why was she bothering to stay? What was holding her on this Earth other than Missy?

She knew it was probably the alcohol doing the thinking, but the crushing pain of never knowing what it felt like to be with her Flame was so strong, Lisa just needed to do something to make it stop.

She found herself in the kitchen opening the cutlery drawer without thinking too much about it. She took out a knife, and was about to touch the sharp tip to her skin when her phone rang, making her jump and drop the knife on the tiled floor. She was shaken out of her drunken depression and she blinked, tears filling her eyes. Had she seriously just been about to end her life, go home to the Angels, all because she couldn't be with the man she loved?

She got to her phone just as it stopped ringing. She picked it up, and checked the number. It was Greg. She called back, and he sounded relieved to hear her voice when he picked up on the second ring.

"Happy New Year," Lisa said, trying to sound cheerful and failing.

"Happy New Year," Greg replied. "Are you okay?"

Lisa took a deep breath and nodded, then realised he wouldn't be able to see her. "Yes, I think so. Feeling a bit down, but I'm okay. Going to go to bed now."

"Okay, well come on over tomorrow, it will just be Violet, me and Julie."

Lisa appreciated him giving her a heads-up that Joseph wouldn't be there.

"Okay, I'll see you tomorrow, thank you for calling."

She hung up, knowing that he may well have saved her life. Lisa switched all the lights off and got a cup of tea to try and limit her hangover the next day, then she retreated to her bed with a hot water bottle. Her mind was whirring too much to fall asleep, so she grabbed her journal and began to spill out her feelings onto the page, hopeful that she might find a way to heal the pain she felt.

When the sunlight shone onto her face the next morning, Lisa winced and blinked, her head feeling like she had repeatedly smashed it against a brick wall. *New Year's resolution number one,* she thought to herself, *no more drinking.*

She opened her eyes fully and noticed that her bedside lamp was still on, and her journal and pen were still on her lap. She saw that the ink from the pen had soaked into her duvet cover and she swore.

She grabbed her phone and peered at the time. It was nearly midday. Slowly, so her head didn't start to spin, she eased out of her bed and made her way to the bathroom. After a cleansing hot shower, her head was beginning to clear a little. She got dressed, and went to the kitchen where poor Missy was waiting patiently for her breakfast. She fed her first, then downed a pint of water and some paracetamol to get rid of the lingering headache. She didn't like to take painkillers if she could avoid it, but she hated headaches, and she didn't want to feel fuzzy; she wanted to go to Violet and Greg's and pitch them the idea she'd had the night before.

She picked up the knife from the floor where she'd dropped it and rinsed it before putting it away. There would be no more incidents like that again. After all, what would happen to Missy if she left? She rubbed her favourite girl behind her ears, and then got ready to go out.

When she arrived in the woods, she breathed in the still, chilly air deeply, listening to the birdsong and a distant plane passing overhead.

Violet greeted her with a big hug and a smile at the door, and she stepped into the cosy house, which was still looking very festive from Christmas.

"Lisa! Happy New Year!" Julie said, getting up to hug her. "You should have joined us last night, it was fun!"

Lisa smiled. "I know, I should have, but Missy and I had fun together."

"Where is Missy?" Violet asked. "You should have brought her over."

"She was happy to stay in and chill. Bless her, she even let me sleep in until nearly twelve."

The women all moved to the lounge, where Greg was reading a book. "Lisa, Happy New Year," he said, getting up to give her a hug. "Are you okay?"

He looked into her eyes and Lisa shook her head a tiny bit. He nodded, but didn't say anything. He went to put the kettle on, and once they all had mugs of tea and slabs of Christmas cake in front of them, Lisa decided to pitch her idea.

"I know that you already do a retreat aimed at Flames who are not together, but I was wondering if you would allow me to run a course for Twins who have actively chosen not to be with their Flame, and how they can focus on their mission and empower themselves to remain strong even when they want to give up."

Violet nodded. "That sounds like a wonderful idea. When I run those retreats, often the main theme is that the Flames are desperate to be with the Twin who has pushed them away or run, and they just want solutions and ideas of how they can be reunited. What you are suggesting is quite different. What kind of programme do you envision?"

Lisa got her journal out of her handbag and flicked to the pages from the previous night. "I think it's important that they learn how to be empowered, to know that even though they are choosing to be away from their Flame, they will still have a connection with them, but by releasing and letting go of the need for them, the attachment to them, they can then fully focus on their mission on this planet. That it is possible for them to move forward, and have a healthy, beautiful relationship with someone who isn't their Flame, but who loves them and will support them in their mission."

"Sounds brilliant," Julie said. "I would love to sign up to that one! I know I won't be with my Flame, and even though it was not my choice, and I have had to learn all of what you describe, it's still hard sometimes."

"Maybe we can create it together," Lisa suggested, feeling excited. "I would love to collaborate with you on it. "

"Sounds like a great plan to me," Greg said. "Let's get on it right away, when do you think you could hold the first retreat?"

Lisa shrugged. "Shouldn't take me too long to get all the material sorted, shall we aim for February?"

"Just in time for Valentine's Day," Violet joked. "Always a good time."

Lisa giggled, feeling lighter and happier with each

moment. She knew that her night of darkness would benefit many Earth Angels who were choosing, as she was, to stay away from their Flame.

*   *   *

"What date did you have in mind?"

Quentin frowned at Jenna, his handful of crisps halfway to his mouth. "Date?" he repeated.

"For the wedding. Spring? Summer? I'm not too keen on autumn or winter weddings, too cold."

Quentin shoved the crisps in his mouth, thinking about how he'd always thought winter weddings were cool. He loved the idea of fur-lined cloaks and mulled wine at the reception. He shrugged and crunched his mouthful.

"You decide," he said after swallowing. "I'm happy to marry you whenever you want. Heck, we could hop on a plane to Vegas tomorrow and make it happen."

Jenna looked over her bridal magazine at him in disdain. "Vegas? Are you serious? Next you'll be suggesting we go to Gretna Green!" She shook her head and buried herself back in the magazine. He hadn't commented on the fact that bridal and wedding magazines had suddenly appeared after Christmas, despite her not having been to the shops.

"We can at least decide on a date for the engagement party," she said, folding down the corner of a page.

"Engagement party?" Quentin echoed. The whole proposing thing was starting to feel like a very costly exercise.

"Of course," Jenna said. "We need to make it official, and besides, our families have never properly met, it would be good to get them all properly acquainted before the big day."

Quentin switched the TV on and nodded. He got the feeling that he would be doing a lot of overtime in the coming months.

"Oh, and do you think we can visit Delia soon? I think my ring needs re-sizing slightly, it's a bit loose."

Quentin nearly spat out the swig of beer he'd just taken, but managed to swallow it, then cough. "What?" he choked out.

"My ring needs re-sizing, can we see that nice sales lady and ask her if she can sort it out for us?"

Quentin's eyes widened in horror. He hadn't foreseen there being a problem with the ring. "Um, uh, I don't know if I'll have time off, um," he stuttered.

"No worries, just give me the receipt, and I'll pop there by myself after work." She looked up and saw his expression. She raised an eyebrow. "Worried that I'll see how much you spent and get annoyed?" She reached over to pat his knee. "Don't be silly, I adore my ring. I don't care how much you spent on it."

He tried to think quickly, but his brain was too fuzzy to be clever. He shook his head. "No, that's not it, it's just, I um, I lost the receipt."

Jenna's eyes widened, but instead of getting annoyed she shrugged. "Okay, well I'll wait until we can go together. But it needs to be soon, I don't want it slipping off my finger by accident."

Quentin nodded, and drank more beer, his fuzzy mind trying to work out how to fix the situation with the extra time he had. The only thing he could do was get Delia to say that they didn't do adjustments and get her to direct them to another jewellers, and then he'd just pay for the changes. Yes. That would work. Though it meant that he would have to sneak off work early again to see Delia.

His stomach flipped, and he knew it had nothing to do with the beer.

CHAPTER EIGHTEEN

"This is it, isn't it? The reason why Gold warned me of the influx of souls going home?"

Pallas nodded, her face sad. "Yes, this is it. And I can tell you now that this was the whole reason for sending you and your team to Earth. So that you could change the fate of the thousand souls who would be coming home."

Pearl shook her head and shifted in the golden chair. "But Gold seemed certain it was a done deal, how did you convince the Elders that we should go to Earth to change it?"

Pallas sighed. "It wasn't easy, I must admit. But once I convinced them that because those on Earth are on a new timeline, any major changes didn't make any difference, they agreed to let us try to change it."

Pearl frowned. "The new timeline. You mean because this is a 'take two', it doesn't really matter? So we can do what we want? Mess with free will?"

Pallas raised her eyebrows. "Well, actually, in the old timeline, this event never occurred. But when Velvet chose to go back, and the new timeline was created, it set off a chain of events that has now created this event. So the Elders agreed that as one of them had created the problem, we could try to solve it."

Pearl shook her head. "This all just seems so confusing. How did Velvet cause this to happen?"

"One of the souls who chose to return to Earth to live their life again has come to the realisation that this is a second take, and so instead of living the honest life they led before, they have decided to go on a path of destruction. They think that it doesn't matter, seeing as the world will end anyway."

Pearl was silent for a moment as she considered this. "Can't this soul be reasoned with? I don't see why we have to handle the situation in this way, if we're messing with free will now, why not just go straight to the source of the problem and sort it out?"

"I know it seems non-sensical, I know that what you're saying is logical, but based on all the possible futures I have seen, the plan as I've laid it out is the best I could come up with." Pallas was silent for a while, and Pearl was aware that the head of the Guardian Angels wanted her to leave.

"I will do my best," Pearl promised, getting up to leave.

"I know you will," Pallas said softly. "Oh, and before you go, Gold has asked if you passed on his message to Starlight yet."

Pearl shook her head. "I gave her the necklace, but I have yet to give her the message, the timing just hasn't seemed right."

Pallas nodded. "I'm afraid you're out of time. You must tell her immediately."

Pearl sighed. "I know." She left the ornate golden room and set off down the path to the lake. Before she could reach it, she awoke and opened her eyes.

The living room was quiet except for Smithsonite's snores, and her own heart beating hard. She now understood why they had been sent to Earth. It wasn't for all the smaller events, the miracle healings or the acts of kindness. It was to stop an event of mass deaths, caused by none other than the Angel of Fate herself. She sighed and slid out of her sleeping bag, and tiptoed out of the room to the kitchen, surprised to see that Sarah was already sat at the dining table, a coffee in one hand an unlit cigarette in the other.

"They're not good for you," she said softly, not wanting to make the Angel jump, though she did anyway.

Sarah smiled and set the cigarette down. "I know. I gave up, I just need to hold one sometimes." She got up to put the kettle on. "You're up early. New orders?"

Pearl thought about her dream and nodded. "Yes. I was also reminded to give you Gold's message," she said quickly before she could talk herself out of it.

Sarah nodded. "I had a feeling you would. What is it?"

Pearl waited until they were both sat down before gathering the courage to say it.

"The Elders wish for you to return."

Sarah frowned. "What do you mean? Gold wants me to come back home, I know that, I feel the pull of our connection every day."

Pearl shook her head. "No, not just Gold. The other Elders. They are worried about several of the other planets in the Universe, and they need you to go back and sort it all out. You're the only one that can, they feel. They have sent teams of Angel volunteers to the other planets, but they are returning home quickly, having found things to be too hostile for them to intervene."

Sarah sat back in her chair and exhaled loudly. "Shit."

Pearl nodded. "Yes. I have resisted giving you the message because I felt awful telling you that you needed to leave your beautiful family, and your life here."

Sarah didn't say anything for a long time. Instead, she picked up the cigarette and lit it. She took a long drag of it, and through the smoky haze, Pearl saw the tears spill from her eyes and hit the wooden table.

"I'm sorry," Pearl said. "I resisted being the messenger, but they gave me no other choice. Without you, the Universe will surely spiral out of control."

Sarah nodded. "Can I return to Earth after?"

Pearl had been expecting that question, and had already asked it herself. She repeated what Gold had told her. "Once home, there will be no desire to leave again."

Sarah shook her head. "I don't believe that. I love my kids, I love my husband. I love my life and my friends and my business. Why on Earth would I not want to return?"

"Because the need to be home will be stronger than your need for your human life. I know you've been here for what feels like a lifetime, but once you return, and you are with Gold again, and you are sorting out the rogue planets, you will be back where you belong."

Sarah sighed and took another drag of smoke before dropping the butt in her cold coffee.

"How long?" she asked, resigned.

"It will happen during our mission. Though you could just leave this planet and go home, there needs to be an explanation for your disappearance. If you come along with us, you can go home when we do."

You're leaving too?"

Pearl nodded. "This mission is the whole reason we have come. Once it is completed, there is no need for us to remain."

Sarah nodded. "When is it going to happen?"

"In a week's time," Pearl said.

Sarah closed her eyes and covered her face with her hands. "There's some people I need to see, things I need to do." She dropped her hands, squared her shoulders and looked at Pearl. "Better get on with it then, hadn't I?"

Despite her bravado, Pearl could see that she was hurting. She got up from her side of the table went over to her friend and wrapped her arms around her. She only had to wait a moment before the Angel began to sob.

*　*　*

"Um, hi, is Louise there?"

Oscar stood awkwardly on the doorstep while the man who'd answered the door – presumably Louise's husband – disappeared into the house and found her.

After a few moments, she came to the doorstep, her eyes wide when she recognised his face, which he knew had changed considerably since they'd last seen each other. She, however, only looked more radiant and beautiful.

"Oscar?" she whispered.

He nodded and she covered her mouth with her hand, her eyes filling up with tears. Oscar's heart broke at the thought of how many tears had been shed due to his heartlessness.

"I'm sorry," he said. "I'm sorry I left, all those years ago. I'm sorry I never wrote. I'm sorry that I didn't realise what we had."

She nodded, tears now streaming down her cheeks. "I'm sorry too."

Oscar frowned. "For what?"

"For not waiting for you," she said softly. "I've regretted my decision since the day you left."

Oscar shook his head. "You did what was right for you at the time, there's nothing for you to be sorry for."

Louise smiled, and wiped her eyes with her sleeve. "So did you." She took a deep breath. "Do you want to come in?"

As tempted as he was, Oscar hadn't wanted to intrude on her life, and was worried about becoming too attached to her again. He shook his head. "I'd better not," he said finally, feeling his heart ache at the disappointment on her face. "I just came to apologise."

He wanted desperately to tell her about the book he'd read about Twin Flames, how he'd realised that was what they were, and how they were meant to be together, to be reunited, so that their love would change the world. But it all seemed too grandiose and unreal. And what was the point of telling her? To make her feel even worse about their breakup? Neither of them were likely to leave their spouses and families. It would just make the situation harder.

"So I guess this is it?" she asked.

Oscar remembered she had said the same thing, so many years before, and an uncomfortable feeling of déjà vu washed over him. "Yes, I guess it is," he said, echoing his younger self.

She nodded, the tears flowing again. "Goodbye, Oscar."

"Goodbye, Louise," he said softly. He turned to walk away before he could leap forward, pick her up and kiss her, smell her scent, and hold her tight to his chest, in the way he so desperately wanted to.

He heard the door close behind him when he was halfway down to the path, but he didn't turn back to look, he kept striding toward his car, and away from the love of his life.

CHAPTER NINETEEN

"These are amazing."

Kirsty beamed at his compliment, and Xander continued to flick through the pages of her sketchbook. She had not only created designs for fabrics, but also some sketches of clothing the fabric could be made into.

"You either need to pitch these to a clothing brand, or you need to get set up making them yourself. Either way, these need to be made into a reality," he said, handing the book back to her. "You can't just keep them to yourself."

"You really think they're good enough? I mean, you don't think it's all just been done before?"

"I think they are amazing, honestly, and I'm not just saying that because I love you, I am saying that because it's the truth." He smiled. "I am about to say something else too, because I think it's time."

Kirsty frowned at the serious tone of his voice and she set her sketchbook to one side. "What?" she asked.

"I think you should move in here with me. There's more room here than at your place. Then I think you should invest all of the money you would normally spend on bills and rent on making your designs a reality."

Kirsty's eyebrows shot up. "Are you serious? I'd have to still contribute here though, I couldn't just live here for nothing."

"Don't be ridiculous, it's not like it will make a big difference to my living expenses. Besides, I'm not in a position where I need it – the readings are going so well at the moment that I've even been putting money aside to make my own dream come true."

Kirsty tilted her head to one side. "Which is?"

"My own psychic café," Xander said. "With homemade food, psychic readings available at all times, a spiritual book corner to lose yourself in, and funky clothing in awesome printed fabrics." He grinned at her and she giggled.

"That sounds amazing."

"I know it does, I dreamed it up, after all," Xander teased. "So what do you say? Will you move in with me?"

Kirsty was quiet for a moment, and Xander wondered if she was still thinking about the whole Twin Flame situation. She hadn't mentioned it since their conversation on Boxing Day, and he'd not mentioned it either, nor the fact that her Flame wasn't on this planet.

After a few minutes, she nodded to herself, then looked at him and smiled. "I would love to," she said. "My tenancy is up at the end of January, I will see if I can give notice to leave then, if not, I will leave end of February, which gives us plenty of time to organise it."

Xander smiled. "Excellent. I think this calls for a celebration, don't you? How do you fancy our favourite coffee shop? Feels like we haven't been there in far too long."

"Done," Kirsty said, jumping up to grab her coat and shoes.

Xander got up a little more slowly, a smile still on his face. Despite the heaviness in his heart, he knew that he had made the right decision to stay with Kirsty and not pursue Astrid.

*　*　*

"Shall I get us some chips?"

Ruby nodded at Lisa. "Yes, please, definitely got a craving for them today."

Lisa grinned. "It's good to be naughty every now and then."

"Definitely," Ruby agreed.

Lisa went down the street to their nearest chippy, and got a large portion for them to share. The last week had been one of her most productive ever, and she was pleased to be back in work. She and Julie had been creating the material for the retreat, and had started to advertise it ready for launching in February.

She got back to the shop, where she and Ruby tucked into their greasy lunch.

"So tell me more about your retreat," Ruby said. "How did you come about the idea?"

Lisa smiled, knowing that she would have to tell her story during the retreat to the participants, and figuring she may as well get some practice. "It's a retreat for Earth Angels who are choosing not to be with their Flames for various reasons and who are choosing to move on with their lives. To have great relationships with other people and follow their purpose and mission. I came up with the idea because it's exactly what I'm doing. I have met my Flame, and I am choosing not to pursue a relationship with him. Instead, I am going to continue with my healing work, and run these retreats to help other Flames in the same situation as me."

"Sounds great," Ruby said. "I think I need to book myself on it!"

"We would be thrilled to have you," Lisa said. "Though I think you have done fabulously well with your business and raising the kids since your Flame left."

Ruby sighed. "I have always been a strong, crazy Faerie. I've always been able to take care of myself, to get everything done, and to make things happen. But I do wish that I could find someone to have a relationship with who would support me and care for me, as well as allow me the space and freedom to be myself. Does that seem like too much to ask?"

Lisa shook her head. "Not at all. We've been taught to think that it's somehow wrong for us to want to be nurtured and cared for, like it's a weak, silly female thing. The time of us women being overly masculine and strong is over. The time for us to step into our power as Goddesses, and for men to step into their power as Warriors, is here."

"Amen to that," Ruby said, waving a chip around. "It's time for the masculine and the feminine to come together into a balanced unity."

"I like that," Lisa said. "I may have to steal that line from you."

Ruby laughed. "Steal away. And book me on the retreat. I need to be there."

"Brilliant," Lisa said. The two women continued eating in an easy silence, and Lisa looked at her phone and saw she only had ten minutes until her next client was to arrive. She always seemed to be very busy at the beginning of a new year, thanks to everyone making resolutions to lose weight, release old baggage and generally make their lives better.

She'd just finished the last of the chips, and was putting the rubbish in the bin, when someone entered the shop. Without even looking up, she knew who it was.

"Good afternoon!" Ruby said, oblivious to her discomfort.

"I'm just going to get ready for my client," she muttered, before turning to leave.

"This is your next client," Ruby said. "His name is Joe."

Lisa finally looked up, and saw Joseph standing awkwardly in the middle of the shop. He looked completely out of place.

"You've booked in for healing?" she asked. Had he not got the message at Christmas?

He nodded, and Lisa sighed. She debated whether to just turn him away, but she was also desperately curious to hear what he had to say.

"Okay, give me a couple of minutes," she said, before going out to the therapy room. She lit some incense, and then tucked a piece of Smokey quartz in her pocket for strength. She called out that she was ready, and she looked up to see him entering the room.

He took off his coat, and slipped off his shoes, leaving them by the door. She motioned for him to sit opposite her, then waited for him to speak.

"I'm sorry to surprise you like this," he started. "I just needed to speak to you, and I was hoping you would be there at New Year's, when you weren't, I figured this would be the only way to see you without it looking suspicious."

"You mean, so that your wife wouldn't get upset?" Lisa said, a little bit of sarcasm sneaking into her tone.

He nodded. "I was worried about you on New Year's Eve, are you okay?"

Lisa frowned. Had he really picked up on her distress? "I'm fine." she said. "No need for you to worry about me. So you're obviously not here for healing, what was it you wanted to say to me?"

He frowned at the clipped, cold way she spoke, and she had to breathe deeply to try and calm her heart which was hammering in her chest.

"I wanted to know if we could be friends, or something. I think of you all the time, and I just want to speak to you, to hear your voice. I'm sorry I kissed you at Christmas, I stepped over the line. I appreciate you wanting to keep a distance because of my wife, but well, I need you."

He wanted to be her friend? Was he serious? With the connection between them? The magnetism and chemistry that crackled and fizzed in the air between their bodies? How could he possibly think that was a good idea?

She shook her head. "I don't think it's a good idea for us to be in each other's lives. I don't think we would be able to resist the pull we feel toward each other. And as I told you very clearly at Christmas, I will not allow you to dump your wife for me, or to have me as your bit on the side. The only sensible thing to do is to say goodbye and to never see each other again."

"And you could do that?" he asked, sadness in his eyes.

"Yes," Lisa said, with confidence that she didn't really feel. "Because there is no way that a relationship beginning in this way, with the destruction of another, can possibly go well."

"How do you know? People break up and get divorced all the time."

"Yes," Lisa said. "They do. I've seen it over and over. And it can destroy lives. Do you have children?"

Joseph shook his head. "No, Joanna isn't able to, and we didn't want to try IVF or adopt, so it's just the two of us."

Lisa nodded. She wasn't sure why she'd asked, though she'd been hoping that he had six children which would make it difficult for him to leave.

"Are you seeing anyone?" he asked.

Lisa frowned. It felt like the more they got to know each other, the more dangerous it would be.

"I don't think we should talk further, it's just going to make things more complicated. I think it would be better if you just left now, and forgot all about me. You've made your commitment to Joanna. I won't be the one to cause your breakup."

Lisa's heart stuttered when she saw a tear run down his cheek.

"There's no chance you're going to change your mind about this?"

"No, there isn't," Lisa said, even though every cell in her being was screaming.

They sat in silence for a few moments, Lisa stared at the gaps in the wooden floor, afraid to meet his gaze that she knew was trained on her face.

"Okay," Joseph said finally. He got to his feet, and went over to the door to put his shoes and coat on.

Lisa finally looked up, just as he was about to leave. "Wait," she said. She got up and went over to him, and her heart broke when she saw the look of hope on his face.

Even though she felt she might regret it later, she also knew she would regret not taking action when she had the chance.

She got close enough to touch him, then tilted her head and closed her eyes. She heard him inhale sharply, then a second later, his lips met hers, and the feeling of finally having come home surrounded her like a warm blanket, and she wanted the moment to last forever.

But this wasn't a romantic, happily ever after film. This was real life.

She pulled away and opened her eyes. She knew from his expression that he'd felt everything she just had.

"Goodbye, Joseph," she said. "Maybe I'll see you again in our next incarnation."

Joseph tried to smile, but couldn't. He opened the door and left, and Lisa heard him talking to Ruby in the shop before leaving. She closed the door and leaned against it, tears running down her cheeks. There was a soft knock a few minutes later.

"Lisa, are you okay?"

Lisa opened the door to see Ruby's concerned face. She shook her head.

"That was your Flame, wasn't it?" Ruby guessed.

Lisa nodded, and Ruby stepped forward to wrap her arms around the Old Soul.

The pain of her heart breaking made her know for certain that it was her mission to help others in the same position. To help lessen their pain.

And somehow, she hoped that it would heal her heart too.

CHAPTER TWENTY

"What do you mean, she doesn't work here anymore?"

The guy behind the counter raised his eyebrow. "I mean, she quit. Is no longer employed here. Has moved on."

The sarcasm was lost on Quentin; he was too busy wondering where Delia had gone and why had she left her job.

"Anything else I can help you with?"

"Do you resize rings?" Quentin asked, still dazed and thinking of Delia.

"No, we don't, but Smythe's just down the road does."

Quentin nodded, relieved that he at least had a legitimate reason not to take Jenna there to get her ring resized.

"Thank you," he said, walking out of the shop, oblivious to the sales guy rolling his eyes.

Quentin walked down the road and into the tiny alley to the tea shop Delia had taken him to. He was hoping that she might be there, and was disappointed to find it empty. In need of something hot and sweet to soothe him, he went up to the counter, and this time, instead of ordering an

Americano, he chose a vanilla latte.

He took his tall glass mug to the same table he and Delia had sat at, and sipped a little of the hot milky drink.

Jenna had talked of nothing but the wedding since Christmas, and though it had only been a few weeks, it was already driving him a little bit crazy. Why was one single day so important to women anyway? He reckoned that if a couple put as much effort into planning their marriage as they did their wedding, there would be far less need for divorce.

He sighed. All of his random ramblings in his mind were just trying to cover up the fact that he was feeling utterly bereft at the idea of never seeing Delia again. He had no idea where she lived, and he now had no idea where she worked. What if she'd left the area altogether?

Quentin looked down at his half-drunk latte. Had he chosen the wrong thing? Was it too late to change his mind?

At that moment, his phone rang in his pocket and he groaned. It was Jenna's ring-tone.

He answered it, knowing that she would only ring again immediately if he didn't.

"Hey, sweetheart," he said.

He listened to her stream of babble, while sipping the rest of his latte. When there was finally a gap, he spoke up. "I'll be home from work soon, shall I bring takeaway?"

Quentin made a mental note of what she wanted to eat, then hung up. He sat in the tea shop and stared at the pictures on the wall for a bit and then finally got up and left. He stopped by the florist to get a bunch of flowers, then went back to his car. He stopped by the takeaway, all the while trying to decide how he could commit himself one hundred percent to the woman he had asked to marry him. He knew that it wouldn't be fair on her, to marry her, if he couldn't give himself wholly and fully to her.

He pulled up outside the house, and looked down at the flowers. The likelihood of him ever seeing Delia again was slim. He had to let her, and their weird connection, go.

He took a deep breath, then let it out. Then he vowed to commit himself and his love to Jenna.

Quentin took another deep breath, grabbed the flowers and the takeaway bag, and got out of the car.

This was the first moment of his new life.

So why did it feel so bleak?

* * *

"We're nearly ready."

Sarah looked up at Pearl and nodded. She was being incredibly calm, and Pearl was amazed at the Angel's strength and resilience.

"I'm not coming."

Pearl frowned at Sarah. "What do you mean?"

Sarah went over to the sink and put her breakfast bowl in it. "For the last week, every night, I have been travelling astrally to the problem planets, and I have been sorting them out. Last night, I had a meeting with the Elders. They see no need for me to rush home. It seems that it was Gold who was pushing for me to go back, and they only agreed to make him happy." She sighed. "I understand his need for me to return, I do, because I too, miss him terribly. But like I told the Elders, there's just too much for me to do here still."

"Wow," Pearl said, leaning against the counter. "I really didn't see that one coming. Though I wondered why you weren't seeing your friends and spending more time with your husband in the last week. I thought perhaps you were just trying to distance yourself in preparation."

Sarah smiled. "No, I was doing whatever it took to remain here. I realised that perhaps I haven't been fulfilling my whole purpose, but that's going to change now. I am going to spend every moment of my remaining life here on Earth doing what I need to make the Golden Age come to pass."

She went over to Pearl and held out her hand.

Pearl opened her own hand, and her heart dropped when she saw what Sarah placed in her palm.

"Please tell Gold that I'm sorry, that I love him, but it's not time yet. I will see him when I'm finished here."

Pearl clasped her hand around the rune necklace, and looked into the Angel's eyes. "Okay, Starlight, I will." Pearl shook her head. "Not looking forward to relaying this message though."

"I'm sorry that you've had to be the messenger of bad news."

Pearl smiled. "I'll survive."

"I'm curious though, your Flame, he's here isn't he, on Earth?"

Pearl nodded. "Yes, he is."

"Have you tried to contact him?"

"No. I admit it was tempting, but it seemed too cruel, considering there was no way we could be together. I knew that this assignment would only be temporary. Besides, he will be home soon enough, I can be patient."

"Maybe you can lend Gold some of that patience," Sarah said wryly.

Pearl chuckled. "Maybe. Well, I'd better get going, thank you, for everything. I hope us being here hasn't put a strain on your relationship. You have a beautiful family."

Sarah smiled. "Thank you." She hugged Pearl tightly. "I'll see you again one day. Peace, love and light be with you always."

"And with you," Pearl replied, tears in her eyes.

She left the kitchen quickly, and returned to the lounge where her team were waiting, all ready to go.

"Let's do it, Starlight is staying here."

The Angels all exchanged glances, but didn't ask any questions.

They stood up as one and left the house, heading for the train station. They needed to travel into the city, where the soul was planning to commit their crime.

Pearl noted that the energy of her peers was high, though there was some nervousness there too. If they failed, many souls would be going home.

They followed their plan down to the last detail, and three hours later found themselves on a red double decker bus. Pearl saw the soul they were looking for, and motioned to the other Angels. His bag was casually placed next to him on the seat, and Pearl knew that the contents were lethal.

They kept a close watch on the man and his black bag, and got off at the bus stop with him, then followed him to one of the city's most iconic structures. Pearl wondered briefly why they couldn't have avoided this completely, remove the bag from him or talk him round. But Pallas had been insistent that she had seen all possible outcomes, and that this scenario would create the least number of casualties.

They followed the man into the building, and noted that he was headed for the fourth floor. "Right," she said to her team. "I'll head straight to the fourth floor. Despite our plan, I would still like to try talking to him. Pietersite, if you can hit the fire alarm and the rest of you, do your best to get as many people out of the building as quickly as possible. Just give me five minutes to go and find him before you hit the alarm. Once the building is clear, if he hasn't detonated it by then, you can come and join me, and we can go home together."

"I quite like it here on Earth. Couldn't we stay as Starlight has?" Smithsonite asked.

Pearl frowned. She hadn't thought about the Angels wanting to remain, she thought they were happy for it just be a short-term mission.

"I would like to stay too," Peridot said.

"Me too," Larimar chimed in.

It seemed they had become accustomed to being human. She could understand how it might be difficult to give it up now after having experienced it. Even she had enjoyed her stay. But she was ready to return.

"If you wish to stay then I cannot stop you. Starlight may be able to help you get set up with a human identity. But I am returning home. If you stay, you're on your own, you will have to make your own way."

Four out of the six Angels nodded eagerly.

"I will return with you," Galena said.

"As will I," Agate said with a nod.

"Make sure you get well clear of the area," Pearl said to

the four. "Good luck, I wish you well."

The Angels nodded, and Pearl took a deep breath and went over to the lift. She got inside, confident that the Angels would follow the plan. She glanced at her watch. She didn't have much time to try and negotiate, but she was going to try her hardest.

The doors opened onto the fourth floor, which was filled with offices undergoing renovations. It didn't take her long to find the right room. She approached the man crouched on the floor over his bag slowly, hoping not to startle him.

"Excuse me, Sir?" she said softly.

He jumped anyway, clearly the adrenalin was pumping through his body. He looked up at her, a little crazed.

"Who are you? What are you doing here?"

Pearl decided to go for the honest approach. "I'm Pearl, I'm an Angel, and I'm here to try and talk you out of detonating the bomb you have in your bag."

His eyes nearly popped out of his head at her words, and then suddenly an ear-piercing shriek filled the air, and he looked around wildly.

"It's the fire alarm," she shouted over the screeching. "The building is being evacuated by my team. I was hoping to be able to reason with you, explain to you why this isn't a good idea, and save your life, as well as any others that get caught up in the fray."

He was shaking his head. "What is going on?" he shouted. "How do you know what I was going to do?"

"I'm an Angel, and I am on a mission from the highest order. They asked me to stop you. Or at the very least, limit the amount of lives lost."

He looked down at the mobile phone in his hand which

Pearl knew was the detonator. She was praying hard that the Angels were clearing the building quickly, she didn't think she would be able to stall him much longer, she could sense he was gathering the courage to set it off.

"I don't believe you!" the man shouted over the noise.

Pearl sighed, she thought this might happen. She closed her eyes and concentrated for a moment. She felt her wings burst from her shoulder blades, and opened her eyes in time to see the man's mouth fall open in shock.

"Do you believe me now?" When the man didn't reply, she sighed. "We can walk out of here," she said. "You and me, and we can get you some help. Otherwise, the only way out of here is to go back home. Thing is, I know that you think it doesn't really matter, because the world is going to end anyway, but consider the ripples you are creating with this action. Consider how the destruction of this building will affect the city as a whole and the energy of the humans living in it? Do you want to create that fear, that pain, that terror?"

Pearl's ears were ringing from the piercing alarm, and her throat was stinging from shouting over the top of it.

Appearing to get over his shock, the man shook his head. "You should leave, you don't need to die too," he said.

Pearl smiled, finding it ironic that he was happy to kill thousands of souls, but he didn't want to harm her. Maybe it was because she was an Angel. "I'm happy to go home. They're waiting for me."

He frowned, and stared down at the detonator.

After another minute, she was aware of two presences beside her, and she saw the man's eyes widen. She glanced either side of her at Agate and Galena. "Empty?" she asked softly, knowing they would be able to hear over the din. Galena nodded.

"Pietersite is just leading out the remaining people. We informed the police and fire brigade of a bomb threat, and warned them not to enter."

Pearl raised an eyebrow. "They listened?"

"We told them we were from the AAT, and we had a highly specialised and trained negotiator already speaking to the subject," Galena said with a smile.

Pearl chuckled, and looked back to the man, who just looked confused now.

"What are you saying?" he screamed. "I don't like people talking about me!" He gripped the phone in his hand and stood up.

Although it went against her beliefs to disobey orders, Pearl decided at the last moment that she would not follow Pallas' instructions, and a moment before the man was able to detonate the bomb, she stepped forward and enveloped him and the bomb in her powerful wings, taking the full impact of the explosion.

"Pearl, it's so good to see you."

Pearl opened her eyes and nodded at Gold, and the Indigo Child by his side. "Gold, Indigo."

She saw Gold look to her side to see the man who had just killed her, a puzzled frown on his face.

"Where are the others?"

"Four in my team chose to stay. I granted them the free will to do so. They would prefer to remain human for a while. I left on my own with him. Agate and Galena wished to return with me, but I changed the plan at the last moment, there was no time to inform them."

"And Starlight?" Gold asked, his right eye beginning to twitch.

In that moment, Galena and Agate appeared in the mists. "Pearl!" Galena said. "That was amazing, there was hardly any damage to the building at all; you completely contained the blast. How did you know it would work?"

Pearl smiled at her fellow Angel, aware that Gold was quietly having a meltdown, waiting to hear about his Twin Flame. "I didn't," she replied. "But I had to try. Galena, Agate, please head to the Angelic Realm, I will be there in a bit." The two Angels nodded and headed away from them, in the direction of the gates.

Gold turned to the Indigo Child. "Can you deal with him, please?" he asked, waving his hand at the man. The Indigo Child nodded, and took the man's hand and led him away.

When they were alone, Gold implored for Pearl to enlighten him.

"Starlight also chose to stay on Earth. She has been doing her work on the rogue planets through astral projection, and the Elders have agreed that she doesn't have to return home in order to fulfil her duties."

Pearl's heart broke at the expression on Gold's face.

"She has chosen to stay," he whispered. "She did not want to return to me?"

Pearl sighed. "Oh, Gold, it's not that she chose her life on Earth over you, it was that she felt that there was more for her to do yet. She hasn't completed her mission there."

Pearl put her hand in her pocket of her robes, and felt the rune necklace there. She took it out and handed it to Gold, who accepted it, tears running down his face.

"She said she was sorry, she loves you, but it's not time yet."

Gold stared at the wooden pendant in his hand. "Thank you, Angel."

Hearing the dismissal in his voice, she nodded then headed home, to the Angelic Realm.

CHAPTER TWENTY-ONE

Oscar was a little nervous, he'd never done anything like this before; would they take him seriously?

He clutched his folder tightly, straightened his shoulders and headed for the main entrance of the prison where he used to work. He was there to present his idea to the board. He was proposing a project that would bring more reading materials to the prisoners that would inspire them, uplift them, and help them to get in touch with themselves.

Even in his head, it all sounded a bit woo-woo for a prison programme, but he was convinced that it could make a huge difference.

He greeted the front desk staff, signed in, went through the usual routine, and finally found himself outside the office of his old boss.

"Oscar! So good to see you! How are things? How's Emily and James?"

Oscar smiled, feeling instantly at ease despite there being three other men in the room who were eyeing him a little wearily.

"Good, we're all great, thank you." He took a seat, and then he took a deep breath before launching into describing his proposed programme. He gave them the statistics of how improved literacy decreased the chances of re-offending, and how inspiring the inmates could help to rehabilitate them. He gave them the lists of proposed books, and also mentioned creating writing programmes, where authors came to visit and set creative writing tasks.

Two of them warmed to it immediately, nodding their heads enthusiastically, and seeming impressed with his figures. But the third one remained miserable. Once he had finished, he asked them if they had any questions or concerns.

"Where exactly do you propose the budget for this will come from? Resources are stretched to the limit as it is. Do you really think that the inmates here, the murderers and rapists and child molesters are really going to be interested in books about Faeries and Angels?" He practically spat out the final words, making Oscar wince.

He pulled out another sheet of paper and handed it to the sour-faced suit. He was glad he'd already considered the costs.

"As you can see, the majority of the costs would be covered by what is called crowd-funding. The prison would only have to contribute a small amount. I'm working on the material for the crowd-funding campaign already."

He raised an eyebrow at Oscar, and handed him back the sheet of paper without a word.

"I personally think it's a fantastic idea," Mick said. "And I know that Oscar here is the perfect guy to run the programme. If there are no objections, I would like to give him the go ahead to do a pilot programme here, for three months, which can then be rolled out in other prisons around the country, depending on its success."

Oscar had to stop himself from grinning. He was so relieved that his old boss thought it was a good idea, that he almost didn't care what the others thought. Though they did have the power to veto it.

He waited anxiously for a few minutes while they appeared to deliberate, then they each shook their heads, making Oscar's heart sink.

"No, no objections from us," the one in the middle said. "I say give it a go."

Oscar sighed in relief, then smiled at them all. "Thank you, I promise I will give it everything I have, I really believe in this."

"I can see that," the middle suit said. "We look forward to seeing the progress reports."

Oscar nodded quickly, gathered up his papers, then shook their hands and thanked them. He stepped outside Mick's office and silently pumped his fist in the air.

"Well done," Mick said.

Oscar spun around, embarrassed to have been caught mid celebration. He lowered his fist and grinned sheepishly.

"I did have one concern, but I didn't want to raise it in there, what about your health? I still cannot have you in the prison around inmates with your condition, has there been any change?"

Oscar nodded, he'd expected that to be an issue. "Yes, before Christmas I had a fit and I fell down the stairs, cracked my head open and nearly died."

Mick's eyes widened. "Shit, I had no idea."

Oscar waved his hand. "Don't worry, I healed up pretty fast once they got me stitched up. Anyway, since then, I've not had a single fit. The fall seems to have knocked it out of me."

"Or given you severe brain damage which has cured it," Mick said sarcastically.

Oscar laughed. "Quite possibly. But anyway, I've had loads of tests, and they can't explain it, but it looks like I'm all good now."

Mick shook his head. "You are one lucky man. How many times have you nearly died now?"

"Too many to count," Oscar said with a smile. "I'll see you soon."

"Yes, and well done, that was a great meeting."

Oscar shook his boss' hand and left the prison, a new spring in his step. He thought about the crazy road that had led him right back where he started, and he couldn't help but wonder if the whole thing hadn't been orchestrated just for him to find his true purpose.

Who knew? Anything was possible.

*   *   *

"I can't believe how perfectly everything worked out," Kirsty said, snuggling closer into Xander's side as they watched the sappy rom-com she'd picked out to celebrate Valentine's Day.

"It did all fall into place very easily," Xander agreed. "But then we did have a lot of Angelic help."

Kirsty giggled. "Even though I totally believe in the Angels, and that you talk to them, it still sounds so funny when you say things like that in normal conversation."

"Normal?" Xander said. "Normal? Please, don't ever use that word in reference to me or us ever again."

Kirsty giggled again. "Is it an insult to spiritual people?"

"It is, it should be considered as a truly blasphemous word."

Kirsty picked up her phone, and flicked through her messages. She suddenly sat bolt upright. "Oh, crap," she said.

"What is it?" Xander's heart started pounding, even though he didn't know what the problem was.

"There was a terrorist attack in London. In the same building where my friend works!"

Xander put his arm around her. "What happened?"

Kirsty quickly googled the information, opened the first article, scanned it quickly then breathed a sigh of relief. "Everyone was evacuated, only the bomber and the negotiators of a special team died in the explosion. The building seems to be intact."

Xander closed his eyes and thanked the Angels. "Well that's good, it could have been a lot worse."

Kirsty finished reading the article and put her phone down. "It really scares me when things like that happen so close to where we are, and where I know people!"

Xander pulled her back into his arms. "There's no need to be scared, I'll take care of you. With the Angels' help of course."

Kirsty smiled and she relaxed back into his embrace. They watched the film for a few minutes, but Xander was acutely aware that Kirsty was deep in thought and not paying attention to the story.

He picked up the remote and pressed pause. "What is it?" he asked.

"I swear you can read me like a book," Kirsty said with a chuckle.

"No, it's more that I can hear the cogs in your brain whirring. What are you thinking?"

"I was thinking about what you said a while back, about wanting to run your own café and also how I want to create my own line of fabric and clothing."

"Okay," Xander said, wondering where she was heading with her thoughts.

"I think we should both do it. I think we should make it happen. Not in the future sometime, but right now. Life's short, we only get one shot at it." She waved her hand to cut off any argument. "I know that we reincarnate and all, but this is our only shot at this particular life, as the people we are. And I think we need to pursue our dreams. Wholeheartedly, unreservedly, and with wild abandon."

Xander grinned. "You aren't going to get any resistance from me on that, I completely agree. If not now, when?"

Kirsty smiled up at him. "There's a great little place that's up for rent in town, I walked past it a week ago."

"Let's look at it on Monday, and see what we think," Xander said, excitement rising up in his chest. He had no idea how they would possibly fund their venture or make it all happen, but it didn't matter. She was right, they had to just go for it. He glanced to his left and saw his Guardian Angel give him the thumbs up and he grinned.

"Brilliant," Kirsty said, grabbing the remote and pressing play again. As the romantic comedy played out on screen, Xander knew that he had made the right choice, and that he and Kirsty would make their dreams a reality together.

*   *   *

Lisa looked around the circle of women, a glowing smile on her face. She couldn't believe that she had managed to gather such a beautiful group of women together to help them with their Twin Flame problems.

"Thank you all so much for joining me on this retreat. Where we all are is a tough place to be, and we each need all the help we can get to not only just survive the separation from our Flames, but to thrive in spite of it."

There were nods of agreement around the group, and Lisa took a deep breath.

"For this first session, I would like for us to each in turn tell our story, about ourselves, our Flames, and anything else that's relevant. My aim is for us to not just go through these exercises and meditations this weekend as individuals, but to connect with each other and form a sisterhood of support, so that when we leave here, we know that we have Angels we can call upon when things get dark."

She took a sip of water, and then began her story. The other women nodded and laughed in the appropriate places, and though she had been nervous about sharing all the details, especially where she'd kissed a married man, she didn't feel in the slightest bit judged by them.

"And so," she concluded, "The chances of us reuniting are slim. Even if he was to leave his wife for completely unrelated issues, I would find it hard to be with him, because I will always see myself the way I saw my dad's girlfriend, who he left my mum for. And I don't want to have those kind of feelings toward myself."

"Never say never," Sarah spoke up softly. "A reunion is not impossible, you may find that you release your feelings around your parents' separation, and that if the opportunity arose where he were single, it would feel good to be with him."

Lisa smiled at Sarah, still slightly in awe that the Angel of Destiny herself had travelled all the way there to attend her retreat.

"Of course," she said. "I will not cut off possibilities in the future, I am open to a reunion, but clearly it wouldn't be possible until I have worked out my own issues."

There were a few giggles around the room, and Lisa smiled at the soul to her right. "Would you like to go next, Delia?"

"Sure," Delia said. "I met my Twin Flame last year, when he was shopping for Christmas gifts for his girlfriend in the jewellers I was working in."

There was a chorus of groans which made Delia smile.

"Yeah, exactly. He was drawn to me, and I could see that he was confused by our connection, but I'm pretty sure that he didn't understand what it was about. I happened to meet his girlfriend, and as much as I wanted to hate her, I couldn't. She was lovely, and I wanted them to make it work. Despite knowing where he lived, I stayed away, and aside from the time he asked me to go for a coffee with him, to talk about his relationship," there were more groans, "I never saw him again. I quit my job after Christmas, when I realised that up until then, I had been living in fantasy land, dreaming of meeting my Twin Flame who was going to sweep me off my feet, and love me unconditionally. I could see that he wasn't anywhere near the level of awareness he'd need to be to even recognise me, and when that bubble burst, I realised that I didn't actually know what I wanted to do with my life. Without the possibility of the dream relationship, I realised I had nothing else in my life worth getting out of bed for." Delia smiled when Lisa reached out to touch her arm in support. "Then I saw this retreat advertised, and I knew that I needed to be here. I want a life, I want to find my passion, and I want to live my purpose here on this Earth. Without my Flame."

Lisa couldn't help herself, she started clapping as soon as Delia had finished and the other women joined in. Delia blushed, looking overwhelmed by the response to her story.

"Thanks," she said shyly when the noise died down.

"Amazing, Delia, thank you so much for sharing that, I hope this weekend gives you the tools and inspiration you need." Delia nodded, and Lisa turned to the next woman.

"What's your story, Astrid?"

"It's very similar to Delia's, though I met my Flame at a Christmas party that he was throwing with his girlfriend. The main difference is that I'm pretty certain that he knew we were Flames, and that he could sense our connection. I'm pretty sensitive to energies, and I could tell that he was closed off to me, that he didn't want to pursue it. Like Delia, I didn't push the issue. He looked happy with his girlfriend, who also seemed lovely." She smiled, but Lisa could see she was holding back tears. "I guess with it being nearly Christmas, I just couldn't bear the idea of trying to split them up. Even if it did mean that I spent Christmas alone with my cat."

Delia reached out and squeezed her knee, and a tear

trickled down Astrid's cheek. "He was just as I imagined him. Or rather, how I remembered him. But I can feel that we won't be together this time. So now I need to work out why I'm here. If it's not to be with him, what's the reason?"

"I'm hoping we'll be able to help you with that," Lisa said. "Because each of you amazing ladies has a very important mission here on Earth, and now is definitely the time to discover it and go for it with everything you have. Now then, Louise, would you like to go next?"

The introduction session lasted nearly two hours, as the women shared their stories, their tears and their fears with the group. By the time they went downstairs for dinner, Lisa already felt like she'd gone through the emotional wringer.

"How's it going?" Greg asked when she entered the kitchen.

Lisa smiled. "Brilliant, the women are all getting on fabulously, and I really think that out programme this weekend will make a big difference."

Greg smiled. "That's amazing. I'm so pleased that you took something potentially destroying and turned it into something so inspiring and healing."

Lisa smiled back and got the plates and cutlery out. "It wasn't easy at first, I must admit, I wanted to curl up into a ball and hide. But then I realised that I am stronger than that, and that it would be waste of another lifetime to hide my gifts and not offer healing to those in need of it."

Lisa jumped then as a pair of arms encircled her waist.

"I think it's inspiring, what you're doing," Violet said in her ear, giving her a tight squeeze. "I know I could have done with your help a few years back," she said, releasing Lisa and going over to Greg to give him a nudge.

"Hey," he protested, waving a ladle. "I can't help it if I'm a slow sometimes."

"A bit slow?" Violet said, disbelief on her face. "Is that what you'd call it?"

Lisa held her hands up in surrender. "Guys, seriously, chill, otherwise I'll have to enrol you both on my retreat, and I don't want to do that. Okay?"

Violet grinned to show she was just messing about and she stood on her tiptoes to kiss Greg. "Sorry, sweetie," she said. "Was only teasing."

"I know," Greg said, kissing her back.

Lisa smiled then sighed. As happy as she was, she still wanted what they had. Would she ever stop wanting it?

When Violet left the room, Lisa turned to Greg. "I keep meaning to ask, what have you and Violet decided to do about having a child? Are you going to see a doctor?"

Greg shook his head. "We've decided to let it be. If it's meant to happen one day, then it will, but if not, that's okay with us both."

Lisa smiled and squeezed his arm, then she joined Violet in serving food to the women who were waiting patiently in the dining room, all chattering away and exchanging war stories.

The meal time was noisy and Lisa enjoyed every minute of it. She felt like she belonged there, with this group of Earth Angels who knew what it felt like to give up on the one person who felt like the perfect fit.

After eating, they all piled back into the workshop room upstairs, and watched a film. Lisa had purposely chosen something sad and romantic, which was guaranteed to make them all cry. She glanced around the room at a particularly harrowing part, and as she had predicted, there wasn't a dry eye in the room. Astrid in particular, was sobbing quietly.

She knew it seemed a bit mean, to make them feel like this, but it was for a very important reason. Once the credits rolled and the music started, Lisa got up and switched it off, then ushered them all into a circle. She looked around at their red faces in the dim candlelight and asked them all to breathe into their pain, breathe into the sorrow they felt.

"Now, I want you to let it go, and know that you don't have to take that pain with you into the rest of your life. I want you to release the pain, thank it for all it's done for you, then let it go. In the gap left behind, shine a bright light, a glowing, beautiful warm light. Shine it into that gap and fill it with love, beauty and strength. You have hurt enough. You have grieved enough. Now is the time to make the decision to move forward, filled with unconditional love for yourself, and for those who love you."

She looked at the group, to see that their faces were already transforming as she watched them release the pain they felt.

"If you need to grieve more, then by all means do it, but you are not allowed to do it alone, you must contact one of us to share it. Never again are you allowed to stay in the darkness by yourself. Do you all promise me that?"

There were affirmative nods and yeses around the small circle and Lisa smiled. "Good. Now go and get some sleep. Tomorrow is the first day of your brand new lives as the amazing, empowered Earth Angels that you are. Good night."

Sarah started clapping, and the others soon joined in. Delia started whooping, and suddenly the noise level went through the roof, and Lisa started laughing. Once she started, she couldn't stop, and one by one the women joined in, until they were rolling around the floor, tears of joy and laughter rolling down their already damp faces.

"It's a good thing we haven't got any neighbours," Violet said from the doorway where she surveyed the scene.

For some reason, her words just made them all laugh even harder.

About the Author

Michelle lives in the UK, when she's not flitting in and out of other realms. She is an avid crafter, and enjoys letterpress printing, knitting, sewing, crochet, photography and many other creative pursuits. She has so far written fifteen novels for adults, one for children, a poetry collection and a self-help book.

Please feel free to write a review of this book. Michelle loves to get direct feedback, so if you would like to contact her, please e-mail **theamethystangel@hotmail.co.uk** or keep up to date by following her blog – **TwinFlameBlog.com.** You can also follow her on Twitter **@themiraclemuse** or on Instagram **@michellegordonauthor**

To sign up to her mailing list, visit:

michellegordon.co.uk

GRATITUDE

A big thank you to all of my beautiful readers who have so patiently waited for this book to be published, your continued support and enthusiasm for the next installment is invaluable to me, and I deeply appreciate every one of you.

So much gratitude to all my beautiful Patreon patrons, who have supported the creation of this book as well as other projects. Thank you Kariel Tejai, Trisha & Bruce Barnes and Vikki Elizabeth Finlay for making generous monthly pledges to help me to continue to create.

Thank you to my beautiful Angel mother, Sally, for joining me on my American adventures this year, bringing the Earth Angel Series to more Earth Angels in the USA. Huge thank you to my stepdad, John, for making it possible.

As always, my amazing friend and editor, Liz Lockwood, deserves a bucketful of gratitude for all the support, help and advice. I love you, Liz.

My genius sister, Liz Gordon, deserves a big shiny gold medal for putting up with my crazy, last minute requests. Her patience is remarkable, as is her continued support.

So much love and light to my beautiful soul sister, Starlight, aka Sarah Rebecca Vine, for inspiring me and helping me through the dark moments.

A big hug and a chocolate frog to my gorgeous twin soul, Tiffany Hathorn, who has continued to cheer me on and help me to be more productive.

Love and hugs to my beautiful new American and Canadian friends, Margaux Joy DeNador, James John Malaniak, Robert Tremblay, Nicole Zaagman, Laurie Huston, Martha Blessing, Paul Ammons, Kellie Fitzgerald, Jonathan Berkowitz, Tracey

Ryan Jastrow, Jamie Rautenberg, Crystal Dawne, Meera Virk & Dirk Terpstra.

Thank you Nicole Brookdale, for your encouragement, and your friendship.

Thank you, Janine Cantin, for producing the Freedom Inside newsletter, which brings inspirational books to prisoners. Your love and dedication to the cause is making a huge difference to the world. To donate to help Janine keep it going, visit FreedomInside.com.

Thank you, Xander, for inspiring one of the characters, and for the use of your name.

Gratitude to my beautiful Faerie friend, Niki, for being there for me with wise advice and awesome hugs.

Thank you, Mr Bee, for inspiring me, and reminding me of my purpose here.

Love as always to my beautiful Twin Flame, Jon. The connection we share continues to inspire me to write, and to fulfil my mission. Thank you, I will love you for eternity.

BOOKS BY MICHELLE GORDON

WHERE'S MY F**KING UNICORN?

Are your bookshelves filled with self-help books, and yet your life feels empty? Do you keep following paths to enlightenment that lead to the same dead ends? You've read the books, attended the seminars and taken heed of every bit of advice going... but you're still waiting for your f**king unicorn to come along! Where's My F**king Unicorn? is a guide to life, creativity and happiness that offers a very different way forward.

Author, Michelle Gordon, explains why, in spite of all your best efforts, your life still doesn't live up to your vision of what it should be, and tells you exactly what you can do about it. In refreshingly down-to-earth language, she shows you how to harness all the self-knowledge you have gained from all those self-help books you've read, and actually start putting it to practical use.

Where's My F**king Unicorn? is published by *Ammonite Press* and is available online and in bookstores.

THE GIRL WHO LOVED TOO MUCH

What would you do if you suddenly found yourself in a different reality that was better for you, but not for those you loved?

Caru loves to make things. And collect things. And give gifts. She loves to print, sew, knit, paint. Her life is full of unfinished projects, yet devoid of financial stability and romance. Though she loves her life, she finds herself disappointing people and struggling to keep everyone happy.

So when Caru wishes life could be simpler, and then finds herself in a completely different world, where her life is easy, money is abundant, and her long-term boyfriend is the most fabulous cook, she can't quite believe her luck.

But will all her wishes come true? Or will the dream turn into a nightmare?

The Girl Who Loved Too Much is a modern day 'It's a Wonderful Life'.

The Girl Who Loved Too Much is published by *Jasper Tree Press* and is available online in eBook and print.

EARTH ANGEL SERIES:

The Earth Angel Training Academy (book 1)

There are humans on Earth, who are not, in fact, human.

They are **Earth Angels**.

Earth Angels are beings who have come from other realms, dimensions and planets, and are choosing to be born on Earth in human form for just **one** reason.

To **Awaken the world**.

Before they can carry out their perilous mission, they must first learn how to be human.

The best place they can do that, is at

The Earth Angel Training Academy

The Earth Angel Awakening (book 2)

After learning how to be human at the Earth Angel Training Academy, the Angels, Faeries, Merpeople and Starpeople are born into human bodies on Earth.

Their Mission? **Awaken the world**.

But even though they **chose** to go to Earth, and they chose to be human, it doesn't mean that it will be **easy** for them to Awaken themselves.

Only if they **reconnect** to their **origins**, and to other Earth Angels, will they will be able to **remember** who they really are.

Only then, will they experience

The Earth Angel Awakening

The Other Side (book 3)
There is an Angel who holds the world in her hands.
She is the **Angel of Destiny**.
Her actions will start the **ripples** that will **save humans**
from their certain demise.
In order for her to initiate the necessary changes, she
must travel to other **galaxies**, and call upon the most
enlightened and **evolved** beings of the Universe.
To save **humankind**.
When they agree, she wishes to prepare them for Earth
life, and so invites them to attend the Earth Angel Training
Academy, on
The Other Side

The Twin Flame Reunion (book 4)
The Earth Angels' missions are clear: **Awaken** the world,
and move humanity into the **Golden Age**.
But there is another reason many of the Earth Angels
choose to come to Earth.
To **reunite** with their **Twin Flames**.
The Twin Flame connection is deep, everlasting and intense,
and happens only at the **end of an age**. Many Flames
have not been together for millennia, some have never met.
Once on Earth, every Earth Angel longs to meet their
Flame. The one who will make them **feel at home**, who
will make living on this planet bearable.
But no one knows if they will actually get to experience
The Twin Flame Reunion

The Twin Flame Retreat (book 5)
The question in the minds of many Earth Angels
on Earth right now is:
Where is my **Twin Flame?**
Though many Earth Angels are now meeting their Flames,
the circumstances around their reunion can have
life-altering consequences.
If meeting your Flame meant your life would never be the
same again, would you still want to find them?
When in need of **support** and answers,
Earth Angels attend
The Twin Flame Retreat

The Twin Flame Resurrection (book 6)
Twin Flames are **destined** to meet. And when they are
meant to be together, nothing can keep them apart.
Not even **death**.
When Earth Angels go home to the Fifth Dimension too
soon, they have the **choice** to come back.
To be with their **Twin Flame**.
The connection can be so overwhelming, that some Earth
Angels try to resist it, try to push it away.
But it is **undeniable**.
When things don't go according to plan, the universe steps
in, and the Earth Angels experience
The Twin Flame Ressurrection

The Twin Flame Reality (book 7)
Being an Earth Angel on Earth can be difficult, especially
when it doesn't feel like home, and when there's a deep
longing for a realm or dimension where you feel you
belong.
Finding a Twin Flame, is like **coming home**.
Losing one, can be **devastating**.
Adrift, lonely, isolated... an Earth Angel would be forgiven
for preferring to go home, than to stay here
without their Flame.
But if they can find the **strength** to stay, to follow their
mission to **Awaken** the world, and fulfil their original
purpose, they will find they can be **happy** here.
Even despite the sadness of
The Twin Flame Reality

The Twin Flame Rebellion (book 8)
The Angels on the Other Side have a **duty** to **help** their
human charges, but **only** when they are **asked** for help.
They are not allowed to meddle with **Free Will**.
But a number of Angels are asked to break their
Golden Rule, and start influencing the human
lives of the Earth Angels.
Once the Angels start nudging, they find they can't stop, and
when the Earth Angels find out they are being manipulated
from the Other Side, they aren't happy.
Determined to **choose** their own **fate**,
the Earth Angels embark on
The Twin Flame Rebellion

THE TWIN FLAME REIGNITION
(book 9)

The **destiny** of many **Twin Flames** is changing.
Those destined to remain apart on Earth are hearing the call to come **together.**
As things begin to shift and change, it suddenly it seems **possible** for them to **reunite,** and have the lives they always **dreamed** of.
But when **visions** and **dreams** of **Atlantis** begin to plague the Earth Angels, and they try to work out their meaning, what they **discover** may jeopardise
The Twin Flame Reignition

THE TWIN FLAME RESOLUTION
(book 10)

When a Seer has a **vision** of the **Golden Age**, she takes drastic action in order to make it happen.
The consequences of her actions are so **epic** that the lives of every **Earth Angel** and every **human** on Earth will be altered **forever.**
As well as the unions of all the
Twin Flames.
She enlists the help of two **Angels** to assist her in
The Twin Flame Resolution

THE OLD SOUL'S HANDBOOK

It's not easy being an Earth Angel on this planet.
I hope the words within these pages help you in whatever
situation you find yourself in.
Simply ask a question or for guidance, and then open the
book to a random page.
The answers are within.

The Earth Angel Series is published by
The Amethyst Angel and is available online in eBook and print.

Visionary Collection

Heaven dot com

When Christina goes into hospital for the final time, and knows that she is about to lose her battle with cancer, she asks her boyfriend, James, to help her deliver messages to her family and friends after she has gone.

She also asks him to do something for her, but she dies before he can make it happen, and he finds it difficult to forgive himself.

After her death, her messages are received by her loved ones, and the impact her words have will change their lives forever.

The Doorway to PAM

Natalie is an ordinary girl who has lost her way. There is nothing particularly special about her or her life. She has no exceptional abilities. She hasn't achieved anything miraculous. Her life has very little meaning to it.

Evelyn is the caretaker at Pam's. The alternate dimension where souls at their lowest point find the answers they need to turn their lives around. The dimension dreamers visit, to help people while they sleep.

One ordinary girl, one extraordinary woman.
One fated meeting that will change lives.

The Elphite

Ellie's life is just one long, bad case of déjà vu. She has lived her life before - a hundred times before - and she remembers each and every lifetime.

Each time, she has changed things, but has never managed to change the ending.

This time, in this life, she hopes that it will be different. So she makes the biggest change of all - she tries to avoid meeting him.

Her soulmate. The love of her life.

Because maybe if they don't meet, she can finally change her destiny.

But fate has other ideas...

I'm Here

When Marielle finds out that a guy she had a crush on in school has passed away, the strange occurrences of the previous week begin to make sense. She suspects that he is trying to give her a message from the other side, and so opens up to communicate with him, She has no idea that by doing so, she will be forming a bond so strong, that life as she knows it will forever be changed.

Nathan assumed that when he died, he would move on, and continue his spiritual journey. But instead he finds himself drawn to a girl that he once knew. The more he watches her, and gets to know her, he realises that he was drawn to her for a reason, and that once he knows what that is, he will be able to change his destiny.

The Visionary Collection is published by *The Amethyst Angel* and is available online in eBook and print.

Not From This Planet is an Independent Publisher on a mission to collaborate with authors to create the best possible books that delight and inspire and entertain – and also pay a fair royalty to the author. They treat every book as if it were their own and they have big have plans to take the publishing world by storm.

Follow Not From This Planet on
Instagram - @notfromthisplanetbooks
Facebook - @notfromthisplanetbooks
Twitter - @ NFTPbooks

NotFromThisPlanet.co.uk